To Tootie

BELLS BOOKS AND MURDER

God's peace and blessings unto you

Jane Svejk

BELLS BOOKS AND MURDER

JANE SVEJK

TATE PUBLISHING & *Enterprises*

Published by Tate Publishing & Enterprises, LLC
127 E. Trade Center Terrace | Mustang, Oklahoma 73064 USA
1.888.361.9473 | www.tatepublishing.com

Tate Publishing is committed to excellence in the publishing industry. The company reflects the philosophy established by the founders, based on Psalm 68:11,
"The Lord gave the word and great was the company of those who published it."

Cover design by Kellie Southerland
Interior design by Joel Uber

Published in the United States of America

ISBN: 978-1-61739-170-5
Fiction / Christian / Suspense
10.09.23

DEDICATION

To all the blessings in my life, especially my husband, Jim, and my sons, Matthew and Christian.

ACKNOWLEDGEMENTS

Thanks are due to the following people, who assisted in the writing of this book: Kathy Walsh, Gloria Ducharme, Bernie Kayan, Karen Duchane, and Diane Dubuc for support, encouragement, proofreading, and steadfast friendship.

Father Steven Frenier and Father Richard Jacob Forcier for their patience, support, encouragement, friendship, and expertise in all things Catholic.

CHAPTER 1

Thursday, June 13, 2003

She sat at the desk, looking out the row of windows facing the church office. Just a few hours ago, the now quiet parking lot had held numerous emergency vehicles. What a way to end her last day of the school year and the final day of a long teaching career.

Father Joe walked across her line of vision, head bowed, slower than usual. Usually he strode quickly across the parking lot between the school and church office, his whole being faith-filled and purposeful. On a mission only he knew. Now it was as if he carried the weight of the world on his shoulders, and she knew nothing she could do or say could lighten the load.

The desk she sat at was a small oak one, passed down by the previous third-grade teacher. There was no doubt in her mind that just as teaching third grade was to be in her past, so would this small piece of furniture that held so many cherished items and memories. Not that she had sat at it much over the years. Whoever would inherit it would probably replace it for something larger. She would not empty its contents today.

Kate Shaw turned slowly to look at the blackboard behind her. It was the old-fashioned black slate kind that had been popular when the school was built almost sixty years before. On it was written well wishes from her class—"Happy Retirement! Have a good summer! Come back soon! Hope to see you next year!" Some were in cursive, some in print, all with pictures of rainbows, hearts, animals, and various other heartfelt decorations.

She stood up and walked over to the windows. It was an effort to even walk, so invasive her grief. As she looked out at her lonely car, the stillness of the building—now void of children, other teachers, and staff—closed in around her. She felt completely alone. A chill went through her body, and she shivered. *I guess I'd better pack up*. It took her only a couple of minutes to put the gifts she had received into two boxes, which stood silently next to a large bleeding heart plant.

"Looks like it will take a couple trips," she said out loud.

Then she heard footsteps coming down the hall. Before she could open her door, it swung open, and in popped Michael, her younger son, and his wife, Elizabeth.

"Hi, Mom, guess you had a rough day today," Michael said as he gathered her into his arms. "We decided you might want to go out for supper tonight even before we heard the news—being your last day and all."

Kate marveled at their thoughtfulness as her eyes filled with tears. "I'm so glad you came," she said as she gave Elizabeth a hug. "I thought the door was locked." It was more a question than a statement.

"Father Joe let us in," Elizabeth replied.

They all picked up a box or the plant and began walking down the hallway to the front entrance since the side entrance was cordoned off with yellow tape.

"I never thought Sacred Heart would be a crime scene," Kate said quietly.

"Was it as bad as it sounded on the radio?" asked Michael.

"I suppose so," said Kate, her eyes suddenly filling with tears. "I'll tell you what I know later."

After they had loaded Kate's belongings into her car and made sure she was all right to drive, Michael and Elizabeth followed her home. They had decided to drop her car off at her house and drive together to the restaurant.

Kate gave Nellie a quick call when they pulled up to her house twenty minutes later. Nellie was an elderly neighbor who lived across the street and just down the hill. Nellie always came over when she saw Kate's car pull into the driveway, and they would have a cup of tea together.

No answer.

She must have gone out with her kids, Kate thought.

The Willow Tree Restaurant was small but elegant. They had eaten there the previous fall when they had celebrated their wedding anniversaries. But that was before her Ted had died. Michael and Elizabeth had made reservations, and they were seated right away in a cozy little corner. Being that it was a weeknight, there was only one other couple at the opposite side of the dining room. Kate was glad that any conversation they would have would not likely be overheard. After the waitress took their orders and brought some wine, Kate took a deep breath and began to tell them about her day.

It had all started out so routinely. Kate had gotten up at her usual time and performed her normal routine of walking up and down her driveway five times before retrieving her newspaper from the newspaper tube on her last time back to the house.

The trees along the driveway were quite full, and the air had that anticipation of a late spring day. Once back inside the house, she had tossed the paper on the table and had set up her coffee pot to brew one cup.

She had laid out her clothes the night before and went right into the bathroom for her morning shower. Afterwards, she had poured herself a cup of coffee, filled a bowl with cereal, and added milk to both. While she ate, she had looked briefly at the newspaper—the obituaries first. It was Ted's anniversary. He had been gone four months now.

Kate had then washed her cup, cereal bowl, spoon, the coffee pot, and the grounds holder and placed them all in the dish drainer. They would dry on their own and be ready to be put away when she got home. Next, she had collected her school things and put a container of yogurt in her small lunch box and was out the door.

She had looked forward to seeing her principal, Al Watson, and having that second cup of coffee with him before the day began. They were the two early birds and would sit in his office, talking about the day ahead or other happenings before the rest of the faculty began arriving. He was easy to be with. He had been a great source of comfort to her over the last few months. Perhaps having lost his wife to cancer, he was more in tune with what she was feeling than others around her. Even that morning he had been trying to talk her out of retiring saying once again the old adage that people who have lost a spouse should never make life changes the first year.

But this move had been in the works since September, and Kate was sure it was the right move for her.

It was only going to be a half day with a prayer service midmorning. She would be giving out the year-end awards and report cards, as well as trying to be sure her students left with all their belongings. She had told them to bring board games to fill up the extra time. She had been sure their excitement would be at an "all-time high." Summer vacation!

Eight o'clock came, and the children had all filed into their room, chatting quietly about what they would be doing all day. They put away whatever sweaters they had and put lunch money on her desk. They would be having a "make your own grinder day," the ingredients of which had already been ordered the day before. Parents bought those ingredients and would be helping them make their lunch at noontime. Community prayer with all the downstairs classes in the hallway had started their day.

The rest of the morning had progressed smoothly. Right after recess and snack, grade three had processed over to church for the prayer service. Kate had been surprised that part of it was dedicated to her. She was given parting gifts, applause, and, of course, a big hug from Father Joe. Tears had come to her eyes as she looked around at all the faces who would no longer be a part of her life on a day-to-day basis.

At this point of her conversation, their dinner came. Elizabeth reached across the table and put her hand on Kate's. "You'll always be able to go back or help out, Mom."

Kate nodded in agreement, taking off her glasses for a minute to wipe her eyes before continuing.

Everyone had gone back to their respective classrooms, and in Kate's class they had begun making and eating their grinders. Al had come in and made one also and sat with her, enjoying the festivities. After all the trash had been collected and the kids had used the bathroom, the parents had taken them out to recess.

Al had gotten up to go and had mentioned to Kate that they should try to get together over the summer for lunch. She had said she really would like that, and he left for his office.

After recess, the parents who had helped with the lunch stayed for the class award ceremony and then, after heartfelt good-byes, left with their children. The eight remaining children had written messages for her on the board and had packed up the last of their things. After afternoon prayers, once again good-byes were said, and the last of her class went out to meet their busses.

Kate had gone up to the teachers' room on the second floor for a cup of tea and was on her way back to her classroom when her longtime friend and colleague met her in the hall.

"Don't stay too long," Jan had said. "I'll be in Monday to give you a hand."

"Don't worry, I won't," Kate answered. She had just begun the ritual of closing windows and pulling down the shades when she heard the commotion.

"I walked toward the door," Kate explained to Michael and Elizabeth, "and heard Al shout, 'You can't come in with that!' Then, an ear-shattering sound rang out. I looked to my left and saw the custodian, John, pull the fire alarm.

"When I looked past him, I saw the back of a tall, heavyset man with bushy hair hurriedly leaving the building by the side door and Mary, the school secretary, kneeling over Al. He was...he was bleeding and...and he wasn't moving, and the bell on the fire alarm was deafening." Kate removed her glasses and bowed her head.

Michael changed seats to be next to her. As he put his arm around his mother's shoulders, she wiped her tears and sat quietly.

Elizabeth was the first one to speak. "Mom, they said on the news that Al died even before the paramedics got there."

"Yes," Kate said. "He must have died instantly. John had the good sense to call the church office, and Father Joe came running over. Unfortunately, it was too late. Of course, the police questioned John, Mary, Father, and me, but none of us had really gotten a good look at the man who shot Al," Kate said quietly.

"After the police questioned us, Father Joe called the other teachers and staff to tell them briefly what had happened. He didn't want them to hear it on the news, I guess."

"Why would someone kill Al?" Michael wondered aloud. "The few times I met him, he seemed like such a nice man."

"That's what the police wanted to know," said Kate. At that, the waitress came to clear the dishes—Kate's was mostly untouched—and Michael asked for the check. They left and rode home to Kate's house in silence.

When they reached Kate's driveway it was almost dark, but Kate noticed that her paper tube was lying on the ground. *I wonder how that happened,* she thought but said nothing. They went inside, and Kate immediately made a pot of decaf coffee and took cups, saucers, and dessert dishes out of the cabinet. Michael and Elizabeth took seats at the table. Kate also got some chocolate chip cookies from the cookie jar and put them on a serving dish.

"Did you have a chance to talk to Andy, Mom?" asked Michael.

"No. He said he'd call tonight." She went to check the caller ID, but although there were a number of calls on there, none were from out of state.

"I'm sure he'll call, Mom. They are three hours behind us in California," said Michael. "He probably hasn't even had time to hear the news."

With a start, Kate realized that Andy, her older son, might hear about the tragedy before she had a chance to tell him herself. But she told herself there was nothing she could do. He was out in California on business but was due home on Friday night.

Kate poured the coffee, set out the milk and sugar, and sat down at the table.

"When will you know the wake and funeral arrangements?" Michael asked.

She shook her head and said, "Not for a while, Michael. Not only did Al not have any close family here, but I would imagine that there will be an investigation of some kind. He and his late wife didn't have any children, and I think they were originally from Minnesota, so any relatives would have to be contacted there. I just can't believe this has happened," she said, her eyes filling with tears again.

Michael and Elizabeth convinced Kate that it might make her feel better if they spent the night. They also decided that Michael would answer any phone calls until she felt ready to talk about the tragedy. As it was, there were four messages on her answering machine, all from people from school. Michael called each of them and explained that his mother was fine but too upset to discuss what had happened. Elizabeth cleaned up the kitchen, while Michael pulled out the sleeper sofa in the small room that served as a guest room and den.

"I'm heading to bed, kids. I just feel so exhausted," she said to them. *Not that I'll get any sleep,* she thought. She did fall asleep, however, but it was a very restless sleep.

Just before five o'clock, a terrifying dream awakened her—one that she had had in the weeks following Ted's death. Just as in all the other nightmares, she saw Ted lying on the outside stairway leading to the basement with his bloodied head resting on the top step, and she was screaming and screaming...

CHAPTER 2

Friday, June 14, 2003

Kate finally got up at 5:30 a.m. She dressed in her sweats and sneakers and went outside. It evidently had showered during the night, because the ground was damp and there were raindrops on her rhododendrons. The air felt fresh. As she walked down her driveway, she decided to say a prayer for Al, his family, and all who would miss him.

She neared her paper tube and found the newspaperman and his car parked by the road. He was hard at work hammering the paper tube pole back in place. Kate waited until he looked up before she said good morning.

"I guess a car must have taken that out yesterday, Tony," she said.

"I don't think so, Mrs. Shaw," he replied. "It looks more like someone deliberately yanked it out. It must have been someone strong." He must have noticed the look of alarm on her face, because he quickly added, "Probably just kids."

He handed her the paper and went on his way. Kate, deep in thought, turned and went back down her driveway. When she reached the house, she laid the paper on the bottom step, turned, and continued her walk up and down the driveway. She couldn't shake the feeling of uneasiness.

As she reached the house on her final lap, she picked up her paper and headed inside. Michael and Elizabeth were still sleeping, so she quietly made coffee then took a cup and the newspaper out onto her deck and sat at the small, round table.

Sure enough, the story of the shooting was on the front page. She quickly put it aside. As she came back into the house, she heard Michael and Elizabeth talking behind their closed door. Michael came out of the den and into the kitchen, and she asked what she could get them for breakfast. He said they would only have coffee, as they planned to stop for breakfast on the way home. Michael had the day off, but Elizabeth had to be in to the doctor's office, where she worked, at noon.

"Did Andy call last night?" Kate asked.

"No, he didn't, Mom. Doesn't he have his cell phone?" asked Michael.

"No, he didn't take it with him because it wasn't working."

"Are you going to be all right here, Mom?" Elizabeth asked. "Michael could stay, and I'll come back for him after work."

Kate hesitated. She wanted to say yes, but she knew they must have things they needed to get done, so instead she said, "No, I'll be fine." They drank their coffee together out on the deck. The sun was up higher in the sky, and Kate was grateful for the large umbrella that shaded the table.

Finally it was time for them to go, and—after collecting the cups, saucers, and spoons and putting them in the sink—Kate walked Michael and Elizabeth out to their car. They had decided that they would come back Sunday and go to church together. By then Andy would be home also. Kate got a hug and kiss from them both, and off they went.

She had just finished washing the dishes and coffee pot when the phone rang. She glanced at the clock. It was nine thirty. It was Andy, and she could tell by his voice that he was upset.

"Have they caught the guy who did this, Mom?" he asked. She told him what she knew and that she was sure no one knew why it happened.

"Don't worry, Andy. This was a terrible shock, but I'll be fine." As he said his good-byes and hung up, the thought crossed her mind that maybe she wasn't so fine after all.

Maybe a hot shower is what I need, she thought. It did help ease the tension in her body. As she was dressing, her phone rang. It was Father Joe, wanting to know how she was. She told him that she was better than yesterday but still somewhat in denial. He agreed. "I know this is sort of short notice, Kate, but I'm calling to see if you would mind meeting with Sergeant Burke and me sometime today. He has some questions for both of us, and I thought it would be quicker if we did it together."

Kate was taken aback but managed to say, "Why don't you both come out to my house, Father? I'm sure we'd have more privacy here."

"Would two o'clock be okay?"

"That should be fine, Father," said Kate. "By the way, I'd be happy to help with the planning for Al's memorial."

"That would be great, Kate. We'll see you at two o'clock."

Kate put on an apron over her clothes and checked to see if she had the ingredients for a carrot zucchini cake. This cake always came out well when company was expected, and Kate didn't have the time or desire to take chances. Once the cake was in the oven, she made her cream cheese frosting. She loaded the dirty bowl and measuring spoons into the dishwasher and wiped off her counter.

Needing to keep busy, Kate vacuumed the living and dining rooms. Then she dusted the furniture. Next, she cleaned the bathroom and put up fresh towels. Lastly, she set out cups, saucers, dessert dishes, silverware, sugar bowl and creamer, and napkins. Looking around, Kate decided all was in order and began to open windows to get some fresh air circulating. Only then did she allow herself to contemplate what possible questions the sergeant could still have for her and Father Joe.

Should I call some of the people who called me last night, or should I wait for them to call again? she wondered. At that point, the timer on her oven went off. She decided that the cake needed another five minutes and closed the oven door. She turned toward her countertop range and put on the teapot. By the time it whistled, her cup with a tea bag was ready, and she filled it with the hot water. She took out the cake and set it on a rack to cool.

When the cake was cool, she frosted it, covered it with plastic wrap, and put it in the refrigerator. She put any remaining dirty dishes into the dishwasher and washed the counter. She took off her apron and put it in the hutch drawer. Then she took a small piece of salmon out of her freezer to thaw out for supper.

A few minutes later, Kate heard the sensor on the driveway beep twice, indicating that someone was coming down the driveway. Once again she thought how glad she was that Ted had installed the sensor before he died. She went out her front door to greet the two men as they got out of Father Joe's car.

Sergeant Sean Burke was a hefty man of average height with a warm, Irish face. His hair was receding and rumpled as if he had a habit of running his hand through it. The uniform he wore was, however, crisp and neat. As he reached out his hand, Kate reminded him that they had met before. He had been the policeman who answered her 911 call the night of Ted's death.

Once they were inside and seated, Sergeant Burke started his questioning by asking them what they knew about Al Watson. Father Joe started by telling him that Al originally came from Minnesota, his wife had died the year earlier, and that they had had no children. Father Joe and Al had gone to college together and were pleased to have been able to rekindle their friendship. He continued giving school information as to when he had hired Al as principal and why he was such a good fit. He told what he knew about Al's past jobs in education. It was obvious from the way he spoke that, not only did they have a good working relationship, but he had considered Al a close friend as well.

"Had Al ever had any kind of problem with any school families, Father?" Sergeant Burke asked.

"Nothing out of the ordinary, Sergeant," Father Joe said hesitantly. "But there was a tuition problem that he worked on for a while that ended with the family leaving the school."

"Can you tell me about it?"

"I don't feel comfortable naming the family, but I'll tell you the circumstances," Father Joe replied. "The family moved into our parish three years ago and enrolled their four children. Needless to say, we were delighted, since we always have an ongoing problem with keeping our enrollment up. They were a great group of kids and fit in beautifully. The mother helped whenever she could, but both parents worked. The only time I saw the father was at Mass on Sunday when they all came together. The first year came and went with no problems, but midway through the second year the father lost his job and couldn't meet the tuition payments. I met with him and essentially wrote off the tuition for the rest of the year and told him not to worry about it.

"This happens from time to time, and we try to help out families who really want to stay. He was sure he would get hired soon, as he had been on a number of promising interviews. Unfortunately, it didn't work out for him, and he was still unemployed when school started this year. Al tried to set up a work program for him to work off the tuition, but he couldn't accept the fact the he wouldn't get a job. They made token payments during this year and then nothing. In April, Al had the tough job of telling them that they couldn't enroll next year. The parents were very upset and pulled the kids out. The whole family stopped coming to church, and I heard that they had moved out of town. Of course, we were equally upset because so many of the faculty had interacted with the family," Father Joe added.

"Can you add anything about that family, Mrs. Shaw?" the sergeant asked, turning to Kate.

"I had their daughter, Emily, in my room this year, and I found the parents to be caring and cooperative up until the second marking period. Emily's grades started to drop, and she began to ask to see the nurse quite often. Both Mrs. Mason, our nurse, and I felt that her home situation was making her anxious. We thought that possibly the parents were not getting along and it was affecting the whole family, especially Emily, who was a very sensitive child. I decided to take Emily aside and talk to her about her grades to see if I could be of some help. She was aware that she wasn't doing as well as in the first marking period. I asked her what she thought was the reason, but she didn't seem ready to confide in me. She did seem concerned that her parents might learn that she was having trouble with her studies. She was willing to stay in at recess time for extra help. She wanted to work it out with me. We did that for a while, but she didn't seem able to concentrate, so I decided that maybe her parents could help or at least tell me if she was having problems with schoolwork at home. I called them in for a conference."

"Was this before they were told they wouldn't be accepted back next year?" asked Sergeant Burke.

"Yes," answered Kate, "but I think they knew that was coming. The father seemed to be a proud man, and he was very upset that Emily wasn't doing as well as she could. They didn't say anything about his being out of work or give me any reason for Emily's academic decline. They both said that they would try to give her more help at home, and our conference ended."

"And did they?" asked Sergeant Burke.

"I didn't see any improvement, but then again, they left soon after that," said Kate.

"Well," said Sergeant Burke, standing up from his seat, "you both have been very helpful. I really can't think of anything else to ask you, but if you think of anything please don't hesitate to call."

Kate watched the car go down the driveway then turned and went into the house. She decided to put all the dishes in the dishwasher instead of washing them by hand. She glanced at the kitchen clock and saw it was four o'clock.

She decided to try Nellie again. Once again there was no answer. *Maybe I'll take a walk up to her house*, Kate mused.

As Kate neared Nellie's house, she noticed that her car was parked in her usual spot. She knocked on the kitchen door but got no answer, so she headed back down the driveway.

By the time Kate got back to her house, she had decided to have a cup of tea on her deck. It was such a nice day. When she entered her kitchen, she noticed that the answering machine was blinking. It was Andy.

"Mom, I'm still in Chicago. The plane to Hartford had some mechanical problems, so it looks like I won't be home until nine or so. I'll pick up something to eat on the way home. I think I'll stay over at your house rather than going to my apartment. See you later. Love ya!"

Kate set up the sleeper sofa for Andy and climbed into bed with thoughts of the meeting with Father Joe and Sergeant Burke filling her mind. After a while, she tried to read a book she had started the day before. Although it was a good mystery, Kate felt herself nodding off and decided to turn out the light.

The noise of a door closing in the kitchen woke her with a start.

"Andy, is that you?" she asked, glancing at the clock and reaching for the table lamp.

"Yeah, Mom, it's me. Anything new about Al?" he asked when he got to her bedroom door.

"No, nothing yet," she answered. "Go ahead and go to bed, hon. We can talk tomorrow."

Kate realized how sad Andy looked. *How the mind does work. I guess sadness is just waiting for an opportunity to surface,* she thought as she felt tears dampen her cheeks. *Dear God, help us to get beyond this.*

It took her a while to fall back to sleep.

CHAPTER 3

Saturday, June 15, 2003

Another awful sleeping night, thought Kate as she slid out of bed. It was 6:00 a.m., and the sun was nowhere to be seen. *Guess it's going to be a cloudy day today.*

Kate went about her morning routine and was just sitting down to read the paper when Andy entered the kitchen. Kate looked up. He had Ted's lean build, sandy hair, and deep blue eyes. Freckles danced across his nose when he smiled. "Well, Andy, what would you like for breakfast?" she asked.

"I'm in the mood for pancakes," he answered, a shy smile flickering across his face.

"Me too!" said Kate, thankful she had an appetite for the first time in two days.

While she put together the ingredients and cooked the pancakes, Andy got out the dishes, silverware, butter, and maple syrup all the while telling her about his trip. It had been his second trip to California.

"I even remembered the Golden Gate Bridge from when we all went out there when I was eight years old, Mom. Of course, I couldn't take in a ball game like when Dad took us."

Kate smiled with the memory of hauling two little kids into that ballpark to see their first major league baseball game. Andy was sure he would catch a foul ball; Michael fell asleep on Ted's lap halfway through the game. *It's so nice to have memories of happier times,* she thought.

Upon hearing the details of Al's murder, Andy shook his head in disbelief. Never could he have imagined that kind of violence at his former school.

"Well," said Andy. "I think I'll be going along, Mom. I want to get home and wash some clothes and write up my report for Monday."

Kate asked him if he would like to go to church with her, Michael, and Elizabeth the next day.

"What time should I be here?" he asked.

"They're coming at nine."

"Okay. I'll see you then," said Andy as he opened the door to leave. Then the phone rang.

"Just a minute, Andy. Let me see who that is, and then I'll walk you out to your car."

Kate looked at the Caller ID and saw it was Nellie's son's number. But it was Nellie's son, not Nellie. "Hello, Mrs. Shaw. How are you?"

"I'm fine, Bob," Kate said, wondering why he was calling. Andy, who had started out the door, stood there half-in and half-out, waiting for his mother. He was surprised to see her face go pale.

Kate reached out and held onto the chair next to the phone. "Your mother's not here, Bob, I thought she was with you."

"No, Mrs. Shaw, she had called me on Thursday afternoon and cancelled her visit. She said she was planning on spending time with you because of the shooting at your school."

"Oh my! I did go up to her house and knock on her door to make sure she had gone. There was no answer, and her car was where she usually parked it. I just assumed that one of you boys came for her." By this time Andy was at her side. "Look, Bob, Andy is here with me and we'll go up there again and break in if we have to. We'll call you as soon as we can."

"I'm going to go there after I call my brother, Mrs. Shaw. It'll take me about an hour, but here's my cell phone number." Kate grabbed a pencil and wrote down the number on the morning newspaper. Bob thanked her and hung up.

Kate grabbed the newspaper, and she and Andy hurried out the door and up the driveway. Neither spoke, but both had similar thoughts: Nellie was elderly and could have had a stroke or heart attack and been unable to call for help. *Oh, Nellie, please be all right*, Kate silently prayed.

Kate was sure they would have to break in because Nellie was usually very careful about locking her doors. She and Andy ran up her driveway. "Try the side door, Andy, and I'll try the front door," Kate said as she started toward the front of the house.

But Andy stopped her in her tracks by yelling. "Mom, it's open!"

A chill coursed through Kate's body.

As they entered the house, Kate hollered Nellie's name with no response. Nellie's kitchen was in perfect order. Dishes were done and arranged in the dish drain. The dish towel was carefully hung on the oven handle. "Well, she's not here, Mom," Andy said. "Do you think she's somewhere outside?"

Just then, Kate passed the cellar door and noticed that it was open—just a crack.

When she opened the door wider and looked down the stairway, she was startled to see two green eyes looking up at her from the darkened basement. Andy was right behind her as she turned on the cellar light. "It's Samantha, Andy! Oh no!" shrieked Kate.

At the foot of the stairs lay Nellie with her cat pressed up against her side. Kate flew down the stairs. As she reached Nellie, she could see dried blood under her head. Her right leg was twisted under her body, and her cheek was pressed against the cold basement floor.

Kate felt for a pulse.

"Andy, she's still alive! Call 911!" screamed Kate.

After Andy had made the call, Kate told him to get a comforter off Nellie's bed and bring it down. Carefully she covered Nellie, all the while talking quietly to her, hoping she could hear. "We've called for help, Nellie. Try to hang on. We're with you now." She could hear the sirens in the distance. But the only sound that came from Nellie was labored breathing.

"Andy, why don't you go out to the road and flag them down when they get here."

"I was thinking the same thing," he replied.

It wasn't more than five minutes until Andy flagged down the ambulance followed by a state police cruiser. He quickly explained where they would find Nellie and that she was unconscious.

When they reached the basement floor, one of the EMTs immediately began checking for vital signs. Andy, Kate, and Samantha stood off to the side watching intently. Then he started an IV. "She's lost quite a bit of blood," he said. "I'm concerned about internal and head injuries. Are you her next of kin?" he asked, looking at Kate and Andy.

Andy answered, "No, we're her neighbors and friends. Her son called us when he was unable to reach her, and we came up to check on her. He last talked to her on Thursday."

"Well," the EMT said, "we're going to splint her leg; it looks broken in more than one place." Then he spoke to the other EMT, "Howard, will you go get what we need from the ambulance?"

At that point the policeman asked Andy and Kate if they had a number to reach Nellie's son. Kate said she did and would call from the upstairs phone. Then Andy and Kate went upstairs.

"Mom," Andy said, "I'll see if I can give Mark a hand with the stretcher," and with that he went back down the cellar stairs.

Kate explained to the policeman that Nellie's son was en route to her house because they had all feared something had happened to her. She dialed Bob's cell phone number, and he picked up right away.

By the time she hung up, Andy, the policeman, and the two EMTs were carrying Nellie's stretcher up the cellar stairs. She was still unresponsive from what Kate could see. Then Kate noticed that Samantha had come up the stairs and was headed for her dish by the sink and began eating. *How amazing*, thought Kate. *That cat stayed by Nellie's side even though she must have been hungry!* Kate petted her and told her what a good kitty she was and quickly hurried out of the house. The men had already put Nellie into the ambulance, and Howard was getting in the driver's side. Kate went up to him and asked, "Can I please ride with her in the back, Howard?"

"Sure."

She was climbing in the ambulance when Andy said, "I'll wait for Bob and come with him, Mom." Mark hopped in and closed the doors.

As they sped to the hospital with sirens wailing, Kate kept talking softly to Nellie, reassuring her that she was there, that her sons would be there soon, that Samantha was okay.

After they wheeled Nellie in, Kate went up to the nurses' station and gave them any information that she knew and told them that Nellie's son, Bob, was en route. She called Nellie's house and told Andy what hospital to come to and then she went to sit in the waiting room.

There were a number of people there waiting to see a doctor. One woman about Nellie's age was sitting with her eyes closed. Kate noticed that she had a bandage around her leg and wondered what had happened to her. There was also a couple with a small baby who was crying. They were speaking to each other in Spanish. Although not fluent, Kate could understand most of what they were saying. The baby was sick and running a fever. They were very worried. Kate sat back in her chair and closed her eyes. *Good time to pray,* she thought.

Just as a nurse came to get the young couple, Andy and Bob arrived. Kate stood up and hugged them both. Then they all sat together, and she told them about her ride here and that Nellie had been taken in right away. Then she told Bob to go to the nurses' desk to tell them of his arrival and sign some papers. Bob soon came back and sat with them. "I called Roger on the way here, but he won't be here for a while, Mrs. Shaw," Bob sadly told Kate. Then the three of them sat together, waiting for some word about Nellie.

Two hours later a very young looking doctor (or so Kate thought) slowly approached them. "Are you folks the family of Nellie Stevens?" he asked. Bob answered that he was her son and that Kate and Andy were long-time family friends.

"We've been able to stabilize your mother, Mr. Stevens," Dr. Moore said after introducing himself. "She is still in a coma, and we're not sure if she will recover. She has a lot of internal injuries, has a fractured skull, a broken leg, and has lost a lot of blood. She must have taken a very hard fall."

Bob explained that Nellie lived alone, and he was unsure when she might have fallen. Dr. Moore said due to her condition, it looked as though it might have happened as long ago as Thursday afternoon. He then said she would be going to intensive care on the third floor shortly, and they could take turns staying with her. He advised them to get something to eat because it would take a while to get her settled.

Bob put in a call to his brother, who was on the way to the hospital, and gave him an update. He also told him that he, Kate, and Andy would probably be in the hospital cafeteria when he arrived.

He told Kate and Andy that Roger should be here in about a half hour. Then the three of them took the elevator to the second floor.

When they reached the second floor they had to ask directions to the cafeteria. They found it to be a well-lighted, large room with a wonderful assortment of salads, hot meals, sandwiches, desserts, and beverages. Even though none of them had an appetite, they all got some fresh coffee and a sandwich. After silently eating for a few minutes, Bob quietly asked about Michael and Elizabeth.

"They're both doing well, Bob," Kate answered. "They like their jobs and their new house. Which reminds me, Andy, will you put a call into Michael and let him know what is going on? We may have to cancel our get together for tomorrow."

Finished with his lunch, Andy left to make his call. Bob and Kate continued to eat and talk quietly about Nellie.

"You know, Mrs. Shaw, my mother never talked about funeral or burial arrangements to me, and I really never gave it much thought." Bob said sadly.

"Bob, let's take it one step at a time. First, your mom's a very strong woman, and if anyone can recover from this, she will. Secondly, if she doesn't, I'll be there to help and I'm sure her many friends will have suggestions. I'm sure she'll want to be buried with your dad, so that's one thing we won't have to worry about. But let's stay positive, okay?" Kate said in the most reassuring voice she could muster.

"Thanks so much, Mrs. Shaw," Bob said with tears in his eyes.

When Andy returned to the cafeteria, he was accompanied by a large, heavyset man with unruly hair. Kate hardly recognized Nellie's other son, Roger. He had put on quite a bit of weight since she had last seen him. She gave him a welcoming hug and they all sat down. Bob caught Roger up on what they knew while Andy got him a cup of coffee. As Roger was finishing his coffee, Nellie's doctor came in looking for them.

"I'm John Moore," he said, shaking hands with Roger. "I have nothing new to tell you about your mother other than she's settled in intensive care now, and you can go up to see her." They all headed out the cafeteria door toward the elevators. All the while Dr. Moore continued to tell them what was known about Nellie's condition. The prognosis was not good. The doctor told them that it was hoped they'd see a positive change within seventy-two hours. If not, there was a good chance there was irreversible brain damage caused by the fall and the loss of blood.

They finally reached the ICU. Bob was noticeably shaken; Roger was stoic. Kate and Andy took a seat outside while Bob and Roger went into the room. There was little to say, so both of them just sat quietly.

Roger was the first to emerge and he sat down heavily next to Andy. "We're going to sit with her in shifts," he said, staring at the floor. "I don't believe this is happening."

Kate asked Roger if he had a chance to eat. "Of course not. I didn't take the time to eat," he snapped at her. Then he profusely apologized for being short with her.

"Maybe you should go down to the cafeteria and get something before they close," Andy said quietly to Roger.

"Yes, maybe I will," Roger said as he got up from his seat. "It's going to be a long night."

Before he turned the corner, he turned back and asked if they wanted him to bring them back anything. Both Andy and Kate said they were fine. "Boy, I've never seen that side of Roger, Mom," Andy said.

"Me neither," said Kate, her eyes welling up with tears. "I'm sure it's because he's so worried."

Time passed, and Bob came out. Despite Bob's assurances that he would call her if there was any news, Kate decided that she would spend the night at the hospital, and Andy would go home and come back for her in the morning. Andy assured her that he would call Michael and Father Joe when he got home. "Be sure to pick up something to eat, Andy," said Kate.

"I will," he answered as he gave her a hug. He and Bob shook hands, Bob thanked him again for all he'd done, and Andy went on his way.

At that point Kate went in to sit with Nellie. She looked up at the clock in the ICU as she pulled up a chair and saw that it was almost 5:30.

"It's all right, Nellie. The boys and I are here," Kate began.

She continued talking to Nellie, reassuring her that everything was going to be okay. She wondered if Nellie could hear her and couldn't help but notice all the machines that were monitoring Nellie's vital signs. Also, Nellie's face was black and blue due to her fall. She had a bandage covering the head wound. Nellie's left leg was in a cast and was in traction. Kate rested her hand on Nellie's and began to pray.

When Roger came back from eating, he came in to relieve Kate. "Talk to her, Roger. She needs to know you're here." Kate said to him.

"You always know what to do, Mrs. Shaw," he said without looking at her, his eyes riveted on his mother. As Kate left, she had the feeling that Roger didn't mean it as a compliment but somehow resented her suggestion.

Around 9:00, Kate came out to find Father Joe talking with Bob and Roger. "Hi, Kate, I thought I'd come by to see if I could be of any help," he said as she approached.

"I was just telling Father what we knew so far, Mrs. Shaw," said Bob. Roger excused himself and went in to sit with his mother, and Father Joe, Kate, and Bob found seats nearby.

"I know my mother would be glad you're here, Father Joe," said Bob. "Even though she's not Catholic, she has a great deal of respect for you and all you do for the school and the community."

"Thank you, Bob, she's a great lady. I've gotten to know her well because she volunteers at the school each week," said Father Joe.

"Yes," said Bob, "she really enjoys reading with the little kids."

"She'll do it again, Bob," said Kate, trying to lift his spirits.

"Why don't we say a prayer together?" suggested Father Joe. He began, "Heavenly Father, send your mercy down on Nellie and her family in this time of need. Our Father..." Heads bowed, Kate and Bob joined in, as did Roger, who had just joined them. As they finished, Kate looked up to see Dr. Moore go into the ICU. They all sat down, waiting and hoping for him to come out with some news.

When the doctor did come out, he told them that they were taking Nellie up to the X-ray department for a CAT scan. He explained that she seemed stable now, but he wanted to make sure there was no swelling on her brain. He also suggested that they go out and get some fresh air and perhaps something to eat. Kate realized then that she hadn't eaten since lunch.

Looking at Bob and Roger, Dr. Moore said, "It will take a while until she is back in the ICU."

"Thank you, Doctor," said Roger. "But I think I'll wait here." Turning to Bob, Kate, and Father Joe, Roger encouraged them to go along without him.

"Father Joe, you know this area better than I do," said Kate as they entered the elevator. "Is anything open nearby?"

"Yes, Kate, there's an all-night diner about a block away, and the food is pretty good," said Father Joe.

When they got outside, Father Joe gave directions to Kate and Bob and excused himself saying that he had the early Mass the next day and needed to get back. Kate and Bob went off in the opposite direction and found the diner without any trouble.

Herb's Diner was small but clean. Booths lined the outside walls. In the center was a counter surrounding all the cooking equipment, grills, and refrigerators. Stools lined the outside of the counter. After taking their seats in one of the booths, Kate and Bob each took some menus that were propped up between the napkin holder and the sugar container. Kate looked at the cover of her menu, and thoughts of Al came to mind. Could two days have passed since his senseless murder? Once again she found herself on the verge of tears and in a state of confusion over why these things were happening.

Bob asked, "Mrs. Shaw, are you all right?"

"It's just that two people very dear to me…" Her voice trailed off into a whisper.

"Remember what you said before, Mrs. Shaw. My mom is a strong person. She'll make it through this if anyone can."

Kate looked at Bob and nodded. She then noticed an elderly man in an apron walking slowly toward them. "Hello, I'm Herb. Can I get you folks something to drink before I take your order?" he asked. Both Bob and Kate ordered coffee. Kate decided on a chef's salad for dinner and Bob, a burger with fries. They were ready to order when Herb returned. After giving their order, Kate asked Herb if he always worked the Saturday night shift.

"I have always preferred working at night," said Herb.

Within ten minutes their orders were in front of them, and they found themselves reminiscing while they ate. Bob talked about his dad and things he and his brother did with him, and Kate talked about Ted and her boys. Bob reminded Kate that his mom had been a widow for almost fifteen years now. Kate told him how his mother had helped her through the last couple of months.

"It must have been quite a shock to find Mr. Shaw the way you did, Mrs. Shaw," said Bob quietly.

"Yes," said Kate. "Ted was always so sure-footed. I still have trouble believing how he died. The thing that bothers me the most is that the accident might not have happened if I had come home from school a little earlier."

"Yes, and I should have tried to talk my mom out of staying home," said Bob. "But you know what Mom always said, Mrs. Shaw. Things happen for a reason." At that point, Herb came over to clear their plates and ask if they wanted any dessert. Both declined but opted for another cup of coffee. Coffee finished, Kate and Bob paid their bill and headed back to the hospital.

As they walked down the street, it began to mist. Kate tried to remember, without success, if she had heard the weather report today. As they entered the doors of the hospital they heard two things—a church bell peeling the midnight hour and a whining, insistent ambulance in the distance.

CHAPTER 4

Sunday, June 16, 2003

As Kate and Bob exited the elevator on the ICU floor, they noticed that Roger was nowhere in sight. Bob took his former seat, and Kate went looking for a restroom. Before she left to rejoin Bob, she splashed some water on her face and combed her hair. Then she hunted around in her purse for a breath mint. "Too much coffee," she muttered as she left the restroom.

She found Roger sitting where she had left Bob. "Any news, Roger?" she asked.

"None to speak of, Mrs. Shaw, although my mother did move her hand a bit," said Roger quietly.

"Perhaps that's a start," said Kate. But Roger said nothing in return. He just looked straight ahead. Kate had noticed when he had looked at her for a split second that his eyes were red-rimmed as if he had been crying. *And why wouldn't he be?* Kate asked herself as she reached over to pat his hand. Although he didn't look at her, he didn't pull his hand away either. They sat like that for a while, both in their own thoughts.

Kate was thinking of happier times such as when Nellie would come into her kitchen to hear about her day. Over a cup of tea Kate would tell her what went on in her classroom that day and listen to Nellie's day as well. *What a dear friend she has become over these last four months*, Kate reflected. Nellie's main content of conversation was usually about her boys. That they had called, when they were coming, the ups and downs in their lives. And of course, her Samantha who was always performing some extraordinary act one would never expect from a cat. *Those moments are what I'd miss the most if Nellie can't make it back*, thought Kate. *She, more than anyone else, brought me back from my despair of losing Ted.*

So deep in thought, Kate didn't realize that Bob had come out of the ICU. He touched her shoulder as he sat down beside her. It was his way of telling her to go in.

As she took up her watch next to Nellie, she decided to continue to talk to her about happy times and she reminisced about their "tea times." She also told her about her plans to go in to school on Monday and begin the job of cleaning out her room. She even told Nellie how much she could use her help. Kate sat by her with her hand on top of Nellie's. She hadn't been there even ten minutes when Nellie made a moaning sound and moved her hand.

Startled, Kate leaned over and grabbed the call button. The nurse on duty came rushing in. She checked Nellie's vitals and told Kate that she was going to put a call into the doctor. As Kate turned to go out to Bob and Roger, Dr. Moore came in and went right to Nellie. Kate quietly left the room.

"I knew it was a good sign when she moved her hand before," said Roger.

"Let's wait until the doctor comes out before we start rejoicing," Bob said quietly. Kate could tell that he was more worried than hopeful.

They all sat down, each staring at the door and waiting for Dr. Moore to emerge.

When he did come out, Kate thought he looked more hopeful. "I think Nellie is coming out of her coma. It will be a while before we know how much damage has been permanent, but her vitals are getting stronger," Dr. Moore said cautiously. Bob turned and hugged his brother and then Kate.

Roger turned to the doctor and said, "Do you think she'll be able to talk to us soon or at all, Dr. Moore?"

"I think there is a good chance now that she will regain consciousness. Other than that, I can't really promise anything. We'll just have to wait and see. She won't be able to talk as long as she is hooked up to some of the equipment, but depending on what happens, we may begin removing some of it. I would advise you to keep doing what you have been—sitting by her and talking to her as if you think she can hear you; she may be able to," Dr. Moore replied.

As the doctor left them, Roger turned and went in to be with his mother, and Kate and Bob returned to their seats. Both felt that their prayers were being answered.

When Andy came off the elevator at 7:00 a.m., the first thing he saw was that Kate and Bob were sitting where he had left them, but Kate was dozing in her chair.

"Andy," said Bob, "my mom is coming out of her coma."

"That's such good news, Bob."

Now wide awake, Kate told Andy she'd like to go in to see Nellie one more time before they left. Nellie was off the respirator and breathing normally, and she looked much better. A few minutes later, Kate and Andy said their goodbyes and left.

In no time they were pulling into Nellie's driveway. Kate jumped out, leaving Andy in the car, and went into Nellie's kitchen. Samantha was curled up in a chair by the window but came by Kate as she rinsed out her water dish, filled it with fresh water, and filled her food dish. Then she cleaned out the litter box and put the new litter in. "There, Samantha," she said as she scratched the top of her head. "That should hold you for a while."

Once back in the car, Andy drove out onto the road toward Kate's house. "Mom, maybe while you're in the shower I'll whip up some breakfast for us," said Andy.

"That'll be great," said Kate.

Kate noticed that it was after eight when they entered her kitchen. After making sure that Andy had everything that he needed, she headed for her bedroom. She decided she would wear her light grey pantsuit and a short-sleeve pink mock-turtleneck. She looked around her bathroom thinking how much she liked the way it had turned out. That was the first thing Ted undertook when he retired in January. It had been unfinished since they had built the house. Something that he was waiting for "time to do." She liked the cheery wallpaper and the white wainscoting. The mauve ceramic tile went along with the rest of the decor. Window treatments, bath mats, and towels all matched.

Once she was freshly scrubbed, she stepped out of the shower and quickly toweled off. She decided to let her small, tight, brunette curls dry on their own.

As she walked out into the hall, she could smell the aroma of fresh brewed coffee mingled with the smell of bacon.

Andy was finishing up cooking some omelets. Kate set the table, took out some orange juice from the fridge, and poured it for both of them. Once Andy served the food and Kate poured the coffee, they both sat down to eat. Kate told Andy what had happened overnight, and he told her what he had done after he had left her at the hospital. Over a second cup of coffee they decided to go to the 10:30 Mass at St. Anne's Church rather than at Sacred Heart, since Kate was sure she'd be bombarded with questions about Al there.

Just then, the phone rang. Right away Kate thought it was the hospital, but it was Michael. She quickly brought him up to speed. Then she asked if he and Elizabeth would still be coming.

"I'm coming, but Elizabeth is under the weather. She thinks she might have picked up an intestinal bug. Needless to say, she is going to stay close to a bathroom." Kate told him of their plans, and he said he would be leaving for her house in about ten minutes and should be there by 9:30.

St. Anne's Church was a massive gothic church that was built in the mid-1800's. It was brownstone on the outside, probably mined in the now quiet Portland quarries. A huge pipe organ was in the choir loft, and as Kate, Andy, and Michael entered the church they could hear the organist warming up. They walked down the red-carpeted center aisle, which was bordered by long, carved pews. Old chandeliers hung suspended from the cathedral ceiling. Floor-to-ceiling stained glass windows depicting bible stories and saints lined the walls. A white marble altar could be seen from afar. This church also had marble altar railings, unusual, since most altar railings had been removed when the church moved from dispensing Communion to kneeling recipients to standing ones after Vatican II.

Although it was almost 10:30, the church was only about half full. Once a thriving French Catholic neighborhood, now it was occupied by those of various other nationalities and faiths causing a drop in attendance. Now only two priests staffed the parish rather than the eight of past years. Because of this, only two Masses were said each Sunday morning instead of a Mass every hour.

Kate, Andy, and Michael genuflected and took their seats about six rows from the front. In the quiet—almost cavernous—church, Kate thought of the recent closures of beautiful churches such as these.

How many weddings, baptisms, sacraments, and funerals have taken place here? she wondered. *And how many generations of the same families sat in these very pews?*

The organist began to play the opening hymn, much louder than during her warm up, and all stood as the altar servers, the lector, and a frail priest slowly walked up the long aisle.

Seemingly before it began, the Mass was over, and Kate, Andy, and Michael were leaving the church and heading for their car.

On the way back to Kate's house, the sun came out, shining brightly, and Kate felt her spirits rise. Andy and Michael stayed for lunch, and while they were eating, the phone rang.

"Hi, Kate," said Jan. "I missed you at church today."

"Hi, Jan. We went to St. Anne's. I really didn't want to answer any questions at Sacred Heart."

"I can understand that."

Kate briefly told her about Nellie then thanked Jan for her call and told her she would see her the next day at school.

Kate and her sons finished eating, and Michael told his mother he was leaving. Kate and Andy walked him out to the car. Andy and Michael talked about getting together for a game of golf, and Kate sent her best to Elizabeth. As Andy walked his mother back inside, he told her that he would be leaving too because he had a lot of paperwork waiting for him at home.

"Let me know any more news on Mrs. Stevens, Mom," Andy said as he gave her a hug on his way out the door.

Kate began to pick up the lunch dishes and put them in the dishwasher, when she heard the driveway sensor signaling Andy's departure. Immediately an image of Ted came into her mind along with an uneasy feeling that there was something about that sensor she should remember. She thought for a moment and shook her head then continued with what she was doing.

She started the dishwasher, wiped off the counter, and headed for the bathroom.

Kate was making her bed when the phone rang. As she hurried to answer it, her thoughts were on Nellie. "Hi, Mrs. Shaw, it's Bob. Good news! My mom woke up. She knew us and even asked for you," said Bob in an excited voice.

"Oh thank God, Bob, I'll be on my way there in about a half hour."

After finishing making her bed, Kate put a banana, a granola bar, and a juice drink into a small lunch box and deciding to wait to call her boys later, headed out the door.

As she backed her car out of the garage she could see that the sun was high in the sky. It shined brightly against a clear blue sky. She took it as a good omen and thanked God again.

Kate had no trouble getting to the hospital and finding a good parking space. As she entered the lobby and headed toward the elevators, she couldn't help but notice how busy it was. One man had a small blond boy in tow. He was carrying flowers, and the youngster, balloons. Another elderly woman with what looked like a man's clothes draped over her arm walked slowly in front of her. All ended up on the same elevator but headed to different floors. The little boy could hardly contain himself. "I'm going to see my mommy and new sister," he announced as the elevator ascended.

"Good for you," Kate answered, noticing not only the happy smiles on father and son but the lack of one on the elderly woman.

The ups and downs of a hospital, thought Kate as she got off on her floor, leaving them on to go to their destinations. The chairs that she and Nellie's son had occupied before were empty, and she thought for a second that Nellie had been moved out of the ICU but realized that that was not the case when she saw Bob emerging from the bathroom down the hall. He greeted her with a kiss on the cheek and a smile. "Roger is in with my mother, Mrs. Shaw. She's asleep more than she's awake, but the doctor thinks the worst is over. They may move her to a regular room tomorrow."

"That's great news, Bob," said Kate, feeling a smile take over her face as well.

"It is," Bob continued, "because Roger will have to return home tonight. He can't take any time off from his new job so he'll have to head back. He certainly didn't want to leave if she was still in the ICU." Bob then told Kate what the doctor had said when he last saw Nellie and what they thought would happen next.

Nellie would have to stay in the hospital until they could get a place for her in a rehab/nursing home because of her leg. Also, the doctor wanted to keep a close eye on her head injury for the next couple of days. Bob also told Kate that the doctor was unsure of what long-term memory or physical problems Nellie would have but was encouraged that she had recognized Roger and himself and had asked for her.

Kate went in and found that some of the equipment that Nellie had been hooked up to was gone. Her leg was still suspended, but her head was raised a bit, and she had more color in her face. Kate began talking to Nellie as she neared her bed and was surprised to see her eyes open.

"Kate," Nellie said as she lifted her hand slightly.

"I'm right here, Nellie, try to take it slowly. We can talk more when you get stronger," said Kate softly. With that Nellie closed her eyes again and fell back into a restful sleep. Kate stayed another ten minutes, but Nellie continued sleeping.

Outside the ICU, Kate told Bob and Roger that she was heading home. They both thanked her for coming and staying and everything else she had done to help. Kate told them she'd be back tomorrow and wished Roger well in his new job and went on her way.

As she drove home, she thought to herself, *I really have to try to go grocery shopping tomorrow. I'm running out of everything.*

She picked up her newspaper when she pulled into her driveway and carried it and her keys into her house. When she had a baking potato in the oven and her salad made, she took out her George Foreman Grill and sprayed the racks with Pam and put some chicken in Italian dressing. Since it would take a while for the potato to bake, she decided to change into her pajamas and robe, put in a quick call to see if Elizabeth was better, and give her an update on Nellie.

The evening news gave little information about Al's death other than it was under investigation, for which she was grateful. Even with the good news about Nellie, she didn't feel like hearing a rehash of the shooting. There was a weather alert, however, about a range of thunderstorms headed her way later in the night.

She thought about how she had loved to lay in bed next to Ted during storms like that and listen to the thunder and watch as the lightening lit up the room. *I always felt so safe,* she thought.

She went into the kitchen to warm up the cooker and set the table, and in no time her supper was ready. No sooner had she eaten, washed the supper dishes, and put them in the dish drain, than the phone rang. Kate glanced at the kitchen clock and saw that it was twenty to eight.

It was Father Joe asking how she and Nellie were and what her plans were for tomorrow, hoping she would be able to come in and help with the planning of Al's memorial. It was her turn to tell him the good news about Nellie. He was pleased to hear the good news. "Will late morning be okay, Father?" she asked the priest. "I want to spend the afternoon with Nellie."

"That will be fine, Kate," said Father Joe. "How about eleven?"

"That sounds good, Father."

"See you then," said Father Joe. "God bless."

He's such a dedicated priest, thought Kate as she hung up the phone. *Too bad some bad apples have cast a shadow over priests like him.*

Kate decided to jot down some thoughts on what to do for the memorial service. She tried to remember what hymns Al had liked and what readings might be appropriate. She would recommend to Father that even though school was out it would be nice if some school children took part in the service. At this point she didn't know whether Father Joe had a memorial Mass or a prayer service in mind. Satisfied with her notes, she folded the paper and put it in her purse. Locking the doors and turning out the lights, she headed for her bedroom.

She picked up her rosary and turned out her lamp. In the dark, she started praying. She made it all the way to the second decade before sleep overtook her.

CHAPTER 5

Monday, June 17, 2003

At 2:00 a.m. the predicted thunder, lightning, and heavy rain woke Kate from a heavy, dreamless sleep. As she lay in bed with her room lighting up and the angels rolling bowling balls, she realized how different this first thunder storm was without Ted. The thought that she would be experiencing many moments like this overwhelmed her, and tears rolled down her cheeks. Up to now, she had been, or maybe kept herself, so occupied that she had warded off such thoughts. But here and now, unprotected from the uncertainties of the future, she felt frightened in a way she hadn't experienced before. Ted had always been there, and before that, her parents. Yes, she had close friends and her children, but somehow she felt vulnerable.

Then she felt her rosary. So many times in the past she retreated to prayer when difficulties arose. She believed that God listens to those petitions sent with a sincere heart. So she picked up where she had left off when sleep overtook her the night before. As she prayed, the storm lessened. She ended the rosary, and slowly sleep once again overcame her.

When she woke at 7:00 a.m., she felt rested and rejuvenated. She put on her sweats and sneakers and headed out for her walk. As she walked up her driveway, she noticed how ferns were starting to grow along the edges. *The rain must have done them good.* In her mind, Kate played over the list she had written the night before and mentally added a few suggestions. She walked up to Nellie's house and let herself in. As if knowing she was coming, Samantha was at the door waiting for her.

Once again she performed the "kitty ritual," getting Samantha set for the day. After some head scratching and kind words, she headed for home, picking up her newspaper on the way.

Back inside her house, Kate walked straight to her purse and got out the list for Al's memorial. She searched for a pen to jot down her latest ideas. After getting ready for the day, Kate walked out on the deck. As she ate breakfast, Kate thought of Nellie and Al, both victims of unfortunate happenings—one a beacon of hope, and the other, of despair.

That hadn't always been the case. Al had offered hope to the future of their small school. The population had grown in the two years he had been at the helm. More importantly, the number of parents involved in the day-to-day workings and fundraising had risen dramatically. He had used excellent judgment in the selection of new teachers, including the woman who was to take over for Kate. How many would miss him?

On a more personal level, Nellie had been a mainstay in her voyage back from the unthinkable. That's the kind of person Nellie was—loyal, honest, hard working, and generous. People could rely on her helpfulness and compassion.

Kate finished her breakfast and came in to wash up the dishes, coffee pot, and strainer. While waiting for her wash to finish, she wrote up a shopping list. *After I meet with Father Joe, I'll go shopping.* The wash was done, so she got her purse and keys, locked up, and climbed into her car.

As Kate was on her way to Sacred Heart, Sergeant Burke and a young trooper, Gerald Snow, were reviewing the latter's report on Nellie Stevens.

"I see here that her son spoke to her that afternoon, and she re-scheduled her visit with him."

"That's right, sir."

"Do we know if she is expected to recover enough to answer questions?"

"No."

"I know you have to be in court this morning, but after that, I'd like you to check with her doctor. See what you can find out."

"I'll do that," replied the trooper.

Kate pulled into the church parking lot and got out. She entered the church, made the sign of the cross using holy water, genuflected, entered a pew, and knelt down. She quietly prayed that she would be able to be of some help to Father Joe. It always amazed her that such a huge building could be so empty yet feel occupied. Somehow, one could always feel comforted. The flickering candles, the statues looking down, the flowers on the altar, all seemed to be waiting for someone to come to place petitions or thanks before an ever-listening Lord.

Kate rose and after genuflecting and blessing herself again, left the church.

She headed toward the church office. Going in, she was greeted by the church secretary, who wanted to know how she was. They were talking as Father Joe came in, and he joined the conversation. "Kate and I are going to go over possibilities for Al's Mass on Saturday, Margaret," he told the secretary. "If anyone calls, please get their number and I'll call them back."

"I'll be sure to do that, Father," Margaret said. Father Joe then showed Kate into his office.

For the next hour they discussed the type of service, the readings, songs, and who would take part. Father Joe told Kate that Al's funeral would take place back in Minnesota. In fact, his body was being readied for the trip as they spoke. He would be buried with his wife. "The family has asked if I would attend, and I intend to do so," said Father Joe quietly. "Therefore the Mass here would be a memorial Mass."

Having the details just about finalized, Kate and Father Joe exchanged stories about Al. Father Joe told her he would contact the other participants in the service. She would do one of the readings. School children would do the others. Kate left, feeling that all had been thought of to make this an appropriate tribute to Al.

As she got in her car, she looked up at the school—now so devoid of activity. Then she left for the grocery store about five minutes away.

By the time Kate pulled into her garage, she felt a headache coming on. She unlocked the doors and brought in her groceries. The teakettle was almost empty, so she put in some water before putting it on the stove to heat up. She worked quickly, and in no time all the groceries were put away. She set up her teacup and poured the now boiling water in. After making her sandwich, she sat down to eat at her kitchen table. As she ate, she finished reading the morning paper.

Sergeant Sean Burke was away from his desk when a call came in from Trooper Gerald Snow. He left a message that he wouldn't be able to get to the hospital to see Nellie because he'd be tied up in court all afternoon.

When he heard the message on his voicemail, Sergeant Burke decided to go to the hospital himself. He figured that even if he couldn't talk to the doctor, he might be able to speak with the family of Mrs. Stevens.

Entering the lobby of the hospital, Sean went straight to the information desk and asked what floor Mrs. Stevens was on. He was told that she was in Intensive Care and only family were allowed to see her. He showed his badge and asked if the woman at the information desk knew who her doctor was. She didn't have that information but would call and see if she could find out. After speaking with the ICU nurses' desk and passing along Sergeant Burke's name, she told him what floor the ICU was on and that the nurse on duty could help him.

After getting off the elevator, Sergeant Burke strode straight to the nurses' station and introduced himself. After hearing his request, the head nurse told him that Dr. Moore was on the floor seeing patients. She told him she would page him, and in a few minutes the Sergeant could hear Dr. Moore's name being broadcast over the intercom. After standing next to the nurses' station for another five minutes, he saw a young man with a stethoscope around his neck walking toward him. *When did doctors get to be so young?* Sergeant Burke asked himself. As Dr. Moore approached, the sergeant held out his hand and introduced himself.

"I'm John Moore," the doctor said. "How can I help you?"

"Well, Doctor, I was hoping you might give me some information on Mrs. Stevens and the extent of her injuries. We're trying to wrap up our investigation."

"Certainly, I'll tell you what I can. Why don't we go into my office," said Dr. Moore as he reached for a file on the nurses' desk.

After they were seated at Doctor Moore's desk, one behind and one in front, Sergeant noticed that the doctor had steel blue eyes and his gaze didn't waver. "In her fall, Mrs. Stevens," the doctor began, "suffered severe injuries to her head and broke her leg in three places. She is still in intensive care now but will be moved to a regular room later today. I have to tell you, Sergeant, that I didn't hold out much hope for her survival when she was brought in. She was unconscious and had lost a lot of blood. Although elderly, she was in good health before her accident, and I think that and prayers have brought her this far and hopefully will help her recover."

"Was there a medical reason for her fall?" asked Sergeant Burke.

"No," said the doctor, "a stroke has been ruled out. There is no way of telling if she had a fainting episode." At that point a clouded look came over his face as if he were struggling with information not yet discussed.

"Dr. Moore, is there anything else you can tell me?"

"I'm not sure, Sergeant, but I have a feeling that Mrs. Stevens's fall may not have been an accident," said the doctor slowly. "When I first examined her, I saw a fairly large bruise on her upper right arm as if it had been grabbed and twisted, not consistent with a fall. But I couldn't tell in what time frame she would have received it. I dismissed it because her family had said, to their knowledge, that she had been alone."

Sergeant Burke thanked him for his time and his willingness to discuss his patient's condition. In answer to his last question, he found out that it would be a while until he might be able to talk to Mrs. Stevens himself. He thought he would try to talk to family members and get permission to go back into her house. He found Bob coming out of the ICU and introduced himself. He explained why he wanted to re-examine his mother's house. Bob, of course, was surprised.

"We just assumed that she had somehow lost her footing or had a medical issue that caused her to fall down the stairs," he said.

"That still may be the case, Mr. Stevens, but it's best to be sure," said Sergeant Burke. Bob, although somewhat shaken to think that his mother's accident was being investigated, immediately agreed to Sergeant Burke's request. He gave him his key to his mother's house.

As Sergeant Burke was getting on one elevator and the door was closing, the door of the elevator next to it opened, and Kate stepped out.

"Mrs. Shaw, I'm so glad you're here! I really need someone to talk to!" exclaimed Bob.

Then he told her about his meeting with Sergeant Burke. "I can't believe anyone would hurt my mother, Mrs. Shaw, but the police seem to have reason to think so."

"It may not be that at all. I've met and talked with Sergeant Burke a couple of times, and I've gotten the impression that he is a very thorough policeman. He probably just wants to rule out the possibility," said Kate. But she thought to herself, *Who would want to hurt Nellie and why*?

As Bob had said, Nellie was moved down to the second floor. She was alone in her room, but there was a second bed. Her bed was next to the window. Amazingly, she slept through the move, so when she did wake up she was somewhat disoriented. Both Bob and Kate were in her room, but it was Bob who spoke to her first. "Hi, Mom, it's Bob. Mrs. Shaw is here too."

"Hello, sweetheart. I'm glad you're here, Kate. Thank you so much for coming. Sorry I can't make you a cup of tea," said Nellie.

"Don't worry, Nellie, you'll be home in no time, and *I'll* be making *you* tea," said Kate, but Nellie was already falling back to sleep.

While they sat quietly waiting for Nellie to wake up again, a nurse came in to check her vitals and suspended leg. She told Kate and Bob that the shift would change soon and another nurse would be in to check. It was hoped that Nellie would be awake enough to start on a liquid diet.

When the next nurse came to check Nellie, Kate and Bob decided to go to the cafeteria for a cup of coffee and something to eat. The cafeteria was somewhat empty, so they were able to get a table by the window once they each got a cup of coffee and Danish.

"What a difference from the last time we were here, Bob, when we didn't know whether your mom would make it or not," said Kate.

"Yes, I feel so much better today. Thank you for keeping my hopes up, Mrs. Shaw," replied Bob. "I just can't believe that anyone would intentionally hurt my mom."

"Did the sergeant say when he planned on going back to your mom's?" asked Kate.

"No, he didn't. I was going to sleep there tonight, but now I think maybe I should get a motel room."

"Maybe the hospital would let you sleep in the extra bed in your mom's room, Bob. If not, why don't you stay at my house—that is, if you don't mind sleeping on a sofa bed?" said Kate.

"Thanks so much for the invitation, Mrs. Shaw," Bob said quietly.

They finished their snack and went back to Nellie's room. She was still asleep, so they took their seats on either side of her bed. They weren't there long when she woke up. "Bob, are you still there?" she asked.

"Yes, Mom, I'm here," Bob said as he got up from his chair. "You gave us quite a scare, Mom."

"I'm sorry, Son, but I'm not seeing very clearly. It seems dark in here." Her room was well lit by the afternoon sun, so Bob looked at Kate with concern all over his face.

"Mrs. Shaw is here too, Mom," Bob told his mother. Kate came closer to Nellie.

"How are you feeling, Nellie?" she asked.

"Right now I feel very tired, and I'm having trouble not only seeing but keeping my eyes open," said Nellie groggily.

"I'm sure the doctor has given you medication to make you more comfortable, Nellie. You have had a serious accident," said Kate reassuringly.

"I really don't remember ..." said Nellie as she drifted back into sleep.

"Don't be concerned," Dr. Moore said from behind. "She'll be like this for a while longer. I don't think this condition will be permanent or long lasting."

Both Bob and Kate gave out a sigh of relief.

Kate stayed by Nellie's side with Bob until almost five o'clock.

Bob found out he could stay overnight with Nellie, so Kate left for home. By the time she was finished feeding Nellie's cat and eating dinner, Kate was too tired to stay up, much less read.

She made sure to lock all the doors, and just as she was falling to sleep, the phone next to her bed rang, startling her. To her somewhat concerned "hello," there was no response, only silence, then the dial tone. Hanging up the phone, Kate decided it must have been a wrong number. *I wish people would just say that*, she thought. She once again was almost asleep when the thought that it might not have been a wrong number crossed her mind, but only for a moment.

Outside her bedroom window, next to her rhododendron bush, stood a solitary figure. He took one of the flowers off the bush, turned, and walked back down the driveway, letting petals of the flower fall to the ground. He threw the stem of the flower on the ground in front of his right front tire as he reached his car. As he drove over it, he smiled and continued on his way.

CHAPTER 6

Tuesday, June 18, 2003

Sergeant Sean Burke and Trooper Gerald Snow drove down the quiet interstate on their way to Nellie Stevens's house. The sun had just broken the horizon and was right in their eyes, so both wore sunglasses. "What do you expect to find that wasn't turned up before, Sergeant?" asked Gerald.

"Maybe nothing," said Sean slowly, "but, then again, it wasn't looked at as a crime scene before."

In no time they were at the exit. As they came down the ramp, they saw a car pulled off to the side of the road with its blinkers on. Trooper Snow pulled the cruiser in back of it and stopped. He entered the license plate in the computer and the information about the car came back indicating that there was no problem, so he got out and approached the driver side of the car. He quickly determined that the driver was lost and, although looking over a map, needed directions, which the trooper gave and went back toward the cruiser. Getting in, he remarked to the sergeant, "I wish all our traffic stops could be that easy." Sean just nodded. They continued a short way and turned down Nellie's road and soon into her driveway.

Both men did a cursory walk around Nellie's house looking for any signs of a break-in. Finding none, they entered the house. They were greeted by Samantha, who decided that they were friendly enough to get a few neck scratches from. Sergeant Burke noticed that her litter box and food and water dishes had been tended to. *Probably Mrs. Shaw*, he thought.

The house seemed in perfect order—no signs of a struggle. "Let's check out the basement, Gerald," said Sergeant Burke as he opened the door and started down the stairs. Other than the blood-stained floor and some pieces of Nellie's slacks that the EMTs had cut away to splint her leg, they found nothing to indicate that anything other than a fall was to blame for her injuries. On the way up the stairs, however, Trooper Snow noticed something on the door jam. A small piece of flannel, had, at some point, been snagged by a tiny nail head.

"I wonder if this could be from someone's shirt, Sergeant. It doesn't look like the type of color an elderly woman would wear. It was probably missed because it is almost the same color as the wood of the door jam," said the trooper. He put the scrap into a plastic bag to be analyzed.

"I think we had better do a house to house to see if anyone saw any strange cars coming or going."

They each took a side of the street and knocked on doors. There was no answer at most of them, since people were probably at work. Although Sean Burke was doing Kate's side of the street, he decided not to question her. He doubted that she would have any information and knew she was grieving. Frustrated by his lack of success, he went back to the cruiser and met Gerald.

"Gerald, I think we need to come back after lunch and try again. Perhaps more people might be home at that time," Sergeant Burke said to the young trooper, who nodded and started up the car.

Back at the station, Sergeant Burke was finishing his second cup of coffee when his phone rang. It was Dr. Moore calling to tell him that Nellie had been moved out of the ICU and seemed to be making slow but steady progress. She had had a good night and was able to stay awake to talk with her son for a while. According to her son, however, she seemed to have no memory of the fall and was somewhat confused as to why she was in the hospital. She also seemed to have some short-term memory loss about other details. The sergeant thanked him and said he would probably wait until tomorrow to come in to question her. The doctor agreed that that was probably the best thing to do and told him he would call if there were any changes.

On Sean's desk he had three files laid out: one was that of Nellie Stevens, another was that of Al Watson, and the third was that of Ted Shaw. Based on his discussion with Nellie's doctor, Dr. Moore, her fall could have been more than accidental. Al Watson, of course, was a homicide.

Then there was Ted Shaw. His death had been ruled an accident, but no one saw him take that fall. The one common denominator was Kate Shaw. Sean noticed that there had been an autopsy done due to the untimely nature of his death. *Perhaps I should talk to the ME and the doctor who did the autopsy,* he thought as he picked up the phone to contact the parties involved.

Unfortunately, the medical examiner could not be reached, but the doctor who had done the autopsy, Dr. Philip Kerr, agreed to meet him at the morgue in an hour.

Sean finished his now lukewarm coffee, wrote a note for Gerald and put it in his mailbox, put the file on Ted Shaw under his arm, and headed out the door.

The morgue always gave Sean the creeps, but it was often part of the job. Oftentimes in criminal cases where a homicide had occurred, a doctor who had done an autopsy on a victim would be questioned and ultimately would be subpoenaed to testify at a trial. Often the doctor could clarify questions about the manner in which the victim died.

Dr. Philip Kerr was a thin man in his early 60s. Although sporting a well-trimmed beard and recent haircut, his clothes looked wrinkled and stained.

"How's it going, Phil?" asked Sean as they shook hands.

Not a man of many words, the doctor answered tersely, "All right. What do you have for me today, Sean?"

Sean handed him the file on Ted Shaw.

"Yes..." Phil said slowly. "I do remember this man. At the time everyone at the scene was sure he had some kind of stroke or heart attack, which caused the fall. But I found him to be a healthy man with no signs of medical cause for the fall. His head wound was ruled the cause of death. It was a jagged wound, which would be expected because his head landed on a jagged cement step."

"Was there anything at all that didn't quite fit, Phil?" asked Sean.

"As a matter of fact, there were a couple of things I questioned at the time," said Phil thoughtfully.

"First, he had on boots that had a deep tread, and those grippers that are used for walking on icy terrain. Frankly, I was surprised that he would have fallen to begin with. I talked to the police who were on the scene immediately after the 911 call, and they said the steps were icy," said Phil slowly.

"Yes, I was one of them," said Sean.

Both men seemed to be caught up in their own thoughts. Finally, Sean interrupted the silence, "You said there was something else?"

"Yes," Phil said, almost hesitantly. "I thought at the time that the head wound seemed larger and deeper than it should have been. But he had been carrying a heavy armload of wood, which could have caused him to fall harder than normal because he couldn't turn to catch himself in any way. I ruled it an accident." With that he handed the file back to Sean.

Sean thanked him for his time and headed back to his car. He called Gerald, and they agreed to meet at a small diner known for fast service and good food. "After we have a bite to eat, we'll finish up our door-to-door on Nellie Stevens's street," he told the trooper.

Over sandwiches, chips, and iced tea, Sean and Gerald discussed their plan for going door-to-door and some other cases they were handling at the time. Sean didn't tell Gerald what had transpired at the morgue.

After lunch they drove to Nellie's street, parked their cruiser, and began their inquiries, each taking one side of the road.

As they had thought, they both found more people at home, but unfortunately, most were of little help. Then Sean knocked on the door of an elderly woman who lived quite a ways up the road from Nellie. After hearing her answers, Sean determined that Anna Northfield was a good friend of Nellie. "Even though Nellie isn't Catholic, we often go together to church on Sundays and go out to either breakfast or lunch, depending on what Mass we go to," she said. Sean could tell that she was upset over what had happened to Nellie, so he told her that Nellie seemed to be out of immediate danger. "I wish I could go see her, but I only drive locally because the highways make me too nervous," she said.

She continued to tell Sean about Nellie and her own family, inviting him to come in and have something to drink. Over glasses of iced tea, she said she hadn't seen any strange cars near Nellie's house that day even though she passed by a couple of times. Of course, she was sorry she couldn't help. Finally, Sean thanked her for the iced tea and her hospitality and rose to leave.

Anna walked with Sean to the door and out onto the stoop. As he started down the walk, she said, "Thanks so much, Sergeant, for telling me about how Nellie was doing. The hospital won't tell people anything these days. I just wish her son had stayed instead of leaving so soon. She might not have taken that fall." Sean stopped and turned to look at Anna.

Kate had had a busy day so far.

She had spent the morning doing her normal cleaning, and she had re-organized her winter and summer clothes. After lunch, she headed outside to do some weeding and hedge clipping. After trimming her azalea, lilac, and forsythia bushes, she headed in for a cup of tea and a snack.

While she munched on some cookies and drank her tea, she decided to mow the lawn. June had been cool this year, and not only were some of her plants late in blooming, but it had taken the grass a while to grow in to the point of needing cutting. She reminded herself again that she needed to find someone to mow her lawn. Ted or the boys had done most all the mowing in the past, and this was her first attempt at it with this lawnmower. She had put it off as long as she could.

There she was, having filled the mower with gas, trying to find out why it wouldn't start, when she heard a car coming down the driveway. When she saw it was a police car, fear coursed through her whole body. *What now?* she thought.

She could see that it was two policemen that she knew—Sergeant Burke and the young trooper who responded to her 911 call for Nellie. "Please don't let it be more bad news, God," she said quietly.

Sean got out of the car first, followed by Gerald. "Hello, Mrs. Shaw, we're just here to see if you could help us with some questions that have come up," said Sean. Kate invited them up onto her porch and offered to get them something to drink. Sean and Gerald took their seats around a round table which was covered with a vinyl floral tablecloth. The cushions on the surrounding chairs matched the tablecloth. Kate went in to get some iced tea, lemonade, and some cookies. She was out in no time, carrying all that she needed on a tray.

She put two pitchers in the center of the table with a plate of cookies and gave each of them a plate, napkin, and glass.

"What can I do for you Sergeant?" she asked Sean.

"How well do you know the Stevens boys, Mrs. Shaw?" asked Sean.

"I've known them as long as I've lived here, Sergeant, why do you ask?" Sean told her about talking to Anna Northfield and what was said about Roger.

"I can't believe that Roger wouldn't have mentioned that he had been here to see his mother before her fall," said Kate, frowning. "Could she be mistaken?"

He told her that Anna was sure the car she saw was Roger's car. He asked her if she knew how to reach him.

"Just a minute, Sergeant. I'll get my address book and give you his number. She came back with it and a piece of paper and pen.

"Nellie wanted me to have their numbers in case anything happened to her. I think very highly of those young men, and I know they were devoted to their mother," Kate said, looking steadily into Sean's steel blue eyes. As she said that, the thought came to her mind of how different Roger had seemed at the hospital. At the time she had chalked it up to being worried about his mother and his job—and she did so again, not telling the sergeant about her observations.

Sean saw the cloud cross over her face quickly. "I'm sure Roger has a legitimate reason for not telling us, Sergeant," she said with conviction.

"Mrs. Shaw, I can't say this doesn't surprise me. But time will tell," Sean said as he turned to leave. Kate walked them out to their car.

"I hope we didn't keep you from your mowing, Mrs. Shaw," he said as they passed by her mower.

"If only I could get the darn thing to start," Kate said.

Sean took a look and found that it had oil and gas, so he tried it himself. Kate noticed that before pulling the cord he pushed the lever to choke. It started right up, surprising Kate.

"Thank you so much, Sergeant. I'd been trying to start it for a good twenty minutes," she said.

"You might have flooded it," said Sean. "If it doesn't start again, let it sit for a while and try again."

"I haven't used this mower before," said Kate, adding that Ted had bought it last summer and that he always did the mowing.

Sean nodded, and he and Gerald got in the cruiser and left. As they went down the driveway, he turned to see that Kate had started mowing her lawn. *Some people just don't catch a break*, he thought to himself. He also decided he would come back again and talk to her without Gerald. *Maybe after she has time to think this over she'll have something to add.*

Kate put the mower in the garage and went inside. She put the teakettle on and set up her teacup. She had some chicken defrosting on the counter for supper but decided to put it in the refrigerator to have the next day. *Somehow I just don't have an appetite,* she said to herself. She made herself an English muffin and took her tea and the muffin over to the table.

After her "makeshift" supper, Kate took a quick shower, dressed, and headed out to the hospital. On the way, she thought about the conversation with Sergeant Burke and decided that she would say nothing to Bob. *The whole thing must have a logical explanation,* she thought.

Nellie was awake when Kate walked into her room, and Bob was sitting in a chair by her bed. She was happy to see Kate, and Kate was happy to see that she was more alert than the previous day.

They spent the next hour exchanging small talk until Nellie dozed off. Ascertaining that Bob was going to spend the night at Nellie's and would see to Samantha, Kate gave him her key and headed home.

CHAPTER 7

Wednesday, June 19, 2003

Kate was up, showered, dressed, and had eaten breakfast when she received her first phone call. It was Jan, wondering what time she was going in to school to do some cleaning out of her classroom. She told her the time, and Jan offered to pick up some coffee for them both.

The ride was only fifteen minutes, but Kate was on autopilot for a good part of it. So much had happened yesterday. She couldn't believe that Roger would have had anything to do with his mother's fall, but the signs were discouraging at best. Both she and Andy had seen the change in him at the hospital. *Who wouldn't be stressed out and irritable under those circumstances?* Finally, she decided to discuss Sergeant Burke's visit with Michael and Elizabeth that night when they came to supper. Surely they would have an objective point of view.

With that plan in place, Kate realized that she had reached the post office. She parked and went in to pick up her mail. Her box was filled mostly with junk mail. She did have a postcard from her good friend, Margot, and her husband. They were vacationing abroad.

No wonder I haven't heard from her! Kate thought as she turned over the "Leaning Tower of Pisa" to read the message. Finding the usual greeting: "Having a great time. Wish you were here," she realized that Margot probably hadn't a clue as to what had happened back home. *Let her enjoy her trip,* she thought to herself.

Back in the car she sorted the junk mail from three bills. One was a tax bill—the first one without Ted—and tears welled up in her eyes. She shook her head and reminded herself that she'd have to stop doing that.

She inched the car out into traffic, turned the corner, went up a short hill, and entered the school parking lot. There she opened the hatch on her car and took out the boxes and the box of trash bags she had gotten when she went grocery shopping and trudged into school.

The side entrance of the school looked normal, certainly not the site of a brutal murder just six days ago. As Kate passed the secretary's office she noticed that the light was on and stuck her head in. Mary was sitting on the floor next to a recycling bin sorting through some papers and looked up as she entered.

Kate was the first to speak, "Mary, how's it going?"

Mary got up, came to her, and gave her a big hug.

Al had hired Mary shortly after he arrived, and she turned out to be an excellent addition to the school. Not only had she been Al's "right-hand" when finances became tight, she took over the lunch program.

Each day at 10:45 a.m. she climbed into her car and went to pick up the hot lunches at the public school. When she came back, she served lunch to the students and faculty in the gym where tables had been set up. There were two shifts—one for the junior high kids and one for the lower grades. The whole school could have eaten at the same time, but although it meant more work, Mary, and Al for that matter, felt that the older kids needed their own lunchtime.

She did all the paperwork mandated by the state too, fitting it in during a day filled with answering the phone and door, occasional subbing, and Al's principal needs. Everyone thought she was indispensable. They knew that she was as dedicated to the school as they were.

At first, Mary had to prove herself. She came in filling the shoes of a beloved secretary, Sally, who had been there for many years and who had outlasted many principals, including two sets of nuns. At seventy, Sally had retired, deciding that she wasn't up to "breaking in" yet another one—Al. But Al had already come broken in, having been a principal at another Catholic school in Minnesota.

Both Mary and Al had been transplants to Connecticut. She was from nearby Rhode Island. She would help him through his beloved wife, Rita's, illness and passing. Never in her wildest imagination would she ever have thought he would meet such an end. She said as much to Kate. "I keep playing it over and over in my mind, Kate, and each time it makes less and less sense," Mary said tearfully.

"I feel the same way," said Kate, tears streaming down her face. "But we'll get through it somehow. Let's go down and make a visit to the church."

Catholic children, especially Catholic schoolchildren who lived in a neighborhood that had a church, were taught at an early age to never pass it by. Instead, they were taught to stop in and say a prayer. Mary and Kate walked together over to the church. Whatever work was ahead of them could wait.

They blessed themselves with Holy Water as they entered, genuflected, and knelt down in a pew in front of the statue of the Blessed Mother. She, too, had lost someone to violence, had seen life-blood flowing from His body, felt helpless, and now was a source of comfort. Mary and Kate left the church less burdened. Only then did Kate tell Mary the reason for her being there and that Jan would be joining her.

Jan did join them as Mary was going back into her office and Kate was collecting her boxes and trash bags. Jan handed Kate her coffee and took one of her boxes and they walked down the corridor to Kate's room. Agreeing to stop for lunch, Jan left for her room, and Kate tackled her file cabinet. She sorted through each drawer leaving some, keeping some in the boxes she had brought, and throwing most away.

The windows in her classroom had been opened early and the shades raised. A mild breeze blew in. June continued to be cooler than normal, for which Kate was grateful. She wanted to be done with her classroom before the really warm weather came.

After the file cabinet, she tackled the bookshelves. They were located under the windows and held an assortment of children's books, teachers' supplies, and classroom supplies. She hadn't gone far when she heard footsteps in the hallway.

It was John pushing a hand-truck carrying some boxes clearly labeled "Saxon Math 3."

The math program was an incremental one with a new skill being taught and presented with already learned skills each day on double-sided worksheets. Practice sheets, timed fact sheets, and teacher instruction materials rounded out the program. Each year, the new daily worksheets had to be organized in labeled files so the teacher could take out a file for the day and have everything she would need for that lesson.

Usually Kate would have had these files all organized by this time, but this year the order came in late. She felt it was just as well because it was probably a good idea for the person who was taking her place to be with her when she filed them.

"Hello, Mrs. Shaw," said John as he entered her classroom. "Look what came for you today. Just what you need!"

John had been at the school longer than anyone else. His own children, now grown, had gone to school there. He had been custodian, handyman, plumber, gardener, and whatever else was needed.

The only other time he had to pull the fire alarm handle was years ago when the furnace had malfunctioned and smoke bellowed out of the basement. At that time the children were led over to the church to safety and to pray for the well-being of their school.

It turned out to be less serious than expected, the furnace was repaired, and life continued on. Everyone knew that it was John who kept that furnace running long past its prime. To replace it might put the school out of business in these hard economic times. Father

Joe's prayers for a rich benefactor hadn't been answered, and the hope of increasing the school's enrollment was dimming with each passing year. The town had a relatively good public school system, and it was free.

John placed the boxes on the counter and left.

Kate glanced at the clock and saw it was almost lunchtime. She decided to give the new person, Nancy Wentworth, a call to set up a date to do the math files.

When she hung up from the phone, she turned to Mary and asked, "Do you want to join Jan and me for lunch at Soup and Nuts?"

"I think I'll stay here and try to get some more done, Kate, but thanks for asking me. I really appreciate it."

After lunch, Jan and Kate returned to the school, and Kate went over to the office to see if she could catch up with Father Joe.

She climbed the steps to the office, knocked on the door, and went in. Father Joe's secretary, Margaret, who was hard at work typing the Sunday bulletin, turned to say, "Oh, hi, Kate. And how are you doing?"

"As well as can be expected. I think we're all just trying to get through this week."

"I know how you feel," said Margaret sadly. "If you're looking for Father Joe, he isn't here today. He had some sick calls that he had to cover for a priest over at St. Elizabeth's parish."

Kate told her that she would be visiting a friend in the hospital but would be home later in the afternoon if he came in and had time to give her a call. As she walked to her car, she tried to shake the disappointment she felt about not being able to talk with Father Joe about Nellie.

The whole way to the hospital, Kate thought about what the sergeant had told her about Roger, deciding that she wouldn't say anything unless Bob brought it up. *I doubt very much that they're going to tell Nellie anything,* she thought as she parked her car in the hospital visitor's lot.

Nellie was not in her room when she got there, but Bob was. He told Kate that she had gone out for therapy. "She goes twice a day. Once for physical therapy and once for occupational therapy." Bob didn't look as tired as Kate had seen him the day before, and he told her he had gotten his first good night's sleep. He smiled broadly as he told her that the usually independent Samantha slept all night curled up next to him.

Kate couldn't really visualize that, knowing Samantha, but said, "I guess she must be lonely, Bob, and she misses your mom."

"I'm sure that's the reason," he said.

After they sat and talked for about twenty minutes, Nellie was brought back in. She was glad to see them but looked tired. Once the aides got her settled back in bed, she asked Kate how long she had been there.

"Only about twenty minutes, Nellie. How are you feeling today?"

"I'm beginning to feel a little better, Kate, I just wish I could remember how I took that fall," Nellie said, looking between Kate and Bob.

"Your doctor said your memory might come back, Mom," said Bob.

Knowing she had to get home to make supper for Michael and Elizabeth, Kate said her goodbyes and told them she would be back the next day.

As she drove home she wondered if Sergeant Burke would talk with Bob about his brother. He certainly hadn't yet. She also realized that Nellie didn't mention Al's murder. *Guess she doesn't remember.* In no time she was pulling into her driveway. She parked her car in the garage and headed into the mudroom and then unlocked her kitchen door.

Once again Kate changed her clothes. That done, she went out into the kitchen and began making the salad. After that, she made some apple crisp and set it on the counter thinking, *I'll stick this in the oven when we start eating and it'll be ready when we finish.* She looked at the clock. Five-thirty. Elizabeth and Michael should be here soon.

She gave Andy a call to see if he'd like to join them for dinner.

Kate went out to her porch and wiped off the vinyl tablecloth. Being out there reminded her of the conversation the day before with Sergeant Burke, and shivers went up her spine. She felt frightened, not just for Roger, but for Nellie and Bob as well. In her heart she knew Roger would never harm his mother, but what *did* happen to her? Just then, the phone rang.

It was Father Joe. "Hello, Kate, Margaret told me that you stopped in. I hope I'm not interrupting your dinner."

"No, Father, Michael and Elizabeth are bringing it, and they're not here yet," she answered.

"Good! What can I do for you?" he asked.

"I was wondering if you might have time to see me tomorrow. I need to get your opinion about something concerning Nellie." Father Joe, always a good listener, could hear sadness mixed with concern in Kate's voice. She told him she was coming to work with Nancy Wentworth the next morning. They agreed to meet right after the seven-thirty Mass. Hanging up, Kate felt so much better.

Elizabeth, carrying some flowers, Michael, and Andy arrived at the same time. After they said their hellos, Andy and Michael went out and sat on the porch, while Kate and Elizabeth went into the kitchen. Kate started to shuck the corn while Elizabeth put the flowers in a vase and brought them out to the table. Then she seasoned the steaks.

In no time dinner was on the table, and Kate put the apple crisp in the oven to cook. As she sat down she looked around at her kids while they said grace. She was so glad that Elizabeth had joined their family while Ted was still alive. That way they could discuss him, and Elizabeth could be included. Also, her presence somewhat filled the empty space left by Molly. Looking at her, Kate thought, *I couldn't love her more if she were my own daughter.*

Andy was regaling them with his work adventures, when the oven timer went off. Kate left them to take out the apple crisp. As she put on the coffee, she could hear them talking and laughing. *They get along so well*, she thought, and pictures of Bob and Roger came to mind. They had always been close.

Kate took some ice cream out of the freezer and placed it on the counter. She had just finished dishing out the apple crisp and scooping out some ice cream on each plate when the phone rang.

Elizabeth was headed out to the porch with cups and saucers as she answered. As Elizabeth was coming back in to get the dishes of apple crisp, she heard Kate hang up the phone angrily. "What's wrong, Mom?" she asked.

"Oh, just another call where no one talks," replied Kate.

"Have you been getting a lot of those kinds of calls, Mom?" asked Elizabeth in a concerned voice.

"No, not really a lot," said Kate, "but they sure are annoying." The two women carried the rest of the things needed for their dessert out to the porch.

Everyone enjoyed the rest of the meal so much that Kate had second thoughts about telling them about Roger. She did tell them that Al's memorial Mass would be on Saturday at ten o'clock, and they decided they would leave from Kate's house together around nine.

Later, as Kate readied herself for bed, she decided she would go to Mass the next morning. One of the things she had loved about teaching at Sacred Heart was going to daily Mass. It was such a great lead-in to her school day. Teaching in a public school with all its restrictions about God just didn't gel with who she was.

Sean Burke sat in his recliner in his darkened living room. He remained there, thinking about what had happened that day. He knew that he should contact Roger Stevens soon to find out why he hadn't been truthful about his mother. But two things kept him from doing so. First, Nellie Stevens was in no danger as long as she was hospitalized, and second, Kate Shaw felt Roger was no threat. He would check up on him, though. *But what did Kate not say?* He asked himself. That, he would have to find out.

CHAPTER 8

Thursday June 20, 2003

The next morning after Mass, Kate waited for Father Joe in the parking lot, and a number of people stopped to talk about Al's murder and memorial. All seemed deeply affected about the loss of such a fine man and appalled that something like this could happen in their quiet town.

Kate was so happy when Father Joe finally came out of church to rescue her from the conversations. Off to the side of the office, which had been a two family house at one time, was a small grassy area with a wrought-iron table and chairs. It was there they decided to sit and have their conversation.

Kate got right to the point, describing what had happened with Sergeant Burke. Father Joe listened quietly.

"I never would have expected to hear anything like that about Roger, Kate," he said solemnly. She agreed then told him what she hadn't told the sergeant about how Roger had seemed at the hospital. "There could be many reasons for him behaving that way, Kate: worry, fear, guilt," said Father Joe.

"I know," said Kate, "but I can't imagine him intentionally hurting his mother."

"He didn't have to hurt her, Kate. Guilt comes in many forms. I'm sure the truth will come out and it will be all right," said the priest thoughtfully.

As they finished up, Nancy Wentworth drove into the lot and waved.

"Well, Father, I guess I'll go along," Kate said to the priest.

Kate and Nancy spent the next two hours arranging the third grade math program. Kate explained how each and every aspect of it worked. Nancy turned out to be a quick study, asking Kate pertinent questions. As they parted, they agreed to meet the following week to discuss other subject areas. Kate left for home with a good feeling about her successor.

Stopping at the nearby store to pick up some needed items, Kate ran into a parent of a former student and couldn't avoid talking about Al. She thought the same thing would happen when she stopped at a nursery to pick up some plants for her flower barrels and was relieved when she didn't know the person who waited on her. As she reached her car, an overwhelming sadness enveloped her. She drove home the rest of the way with tears streaming down her cheeks.

She had just finished putting her groceries away when her phone rang.

"Hi, Kate," said Jan. "What have you been up to today? I've been trying to reach you all morning." Kate told her that she had been working with Nancy. Then Jan suggested she bring lunch over so they could have a chance to talk. If it were anyone else, Kate would have begged off, but she decided she needed company. Jan always had a way of cheering her up.

Jan could tell that Kate had been crying by looking at her friend's eyes. Saying nothing, she put down her lunch items and gave Kate a big hug. Smelling Jan's corn chowder gave Kate's appetite a jumpstart. After heating it up, the two friends carried everything out to the porch. "I've always loved the view from your porch, Kate," said Jan as the two ate their bowls of soup. Kate smiled. She told her all about her morning, leaving out her talk with Father Joe and the crying jag on the way home. Jan, for her part, was glad to hear that Nancy would be easy to work with.

After Jan left, Kate went outside intent on planting her flowers. As she went to the shed, she tried to remember if she did, indeed, have any soil left over from the previous year. When she opened the door on the shed, she was surprised at what she found. She did have soil, but it was no longer in the bag but spread all over the floor of the shed. After looking at the mess and trying to decide what kind of animal could have caused it, Kate went to the garage for a flat shovel and a wheelbarrow. Back at the shed, she shoveled the soil into the wheelbarrow and headed for her planters which were located on either side of her garage.

In no time the flowers were planted, watered, and all the tools were put away. *Thank God, Ted had everything*

I needed, she thought. A moment of sadness washed over her as she remembered that had he still been alive he probably would have been helping her plant.

On going in, she decided on a quick shower before leaving to go see Nellie. Refreshed, she got dressed and put on the teakettle.

Suddenly, a humming bird flew in front of her sliding glass door and hovered. "He's probably trying to tell me I need to refill his feeder," she said aloud. She put her dishes in the sink and took out some sugar and a measuring cup. "Four parts water to one part sugar," she said as she stirred the ingredients together. Then she went out the sliding doors on to her deck and filled the feeder.

It was then that she noticed some lower branches had broken off of her rhododendron bush. The question of what could have happened there only stayed in her conscience thought for a minute. Picking up the branches, she walked over to the edge of her lawn and threw them into the woods. She turned and went in the house, got her things together, locked up, and left for the hospital.

It had been a long day for Sean Burke. He had made quite a bit of progress on some paperwork, had appeared in court to give testimony on a DUI case, and had made some inquiries about Roger Stevens. He learned that Roger had only been at his place of employment for two weeks, after being laid off from his old job two months ago. After speaking to the human resource person at Roger's old company, Sean learned that Roger was well thought of and had been laid off along with fifteen others due to downsizing by a company that was struggling to stay in business. An excellent recommendation had been sent to his new employer. Based on that information, Sean had decided to wait to call Roger's new employer.

On another front, other investigators who had gone door to door interviewing neighbors of the school, had turned up nothing on Al's murder. The killer had timed his strike perfectly. Other than Kate, John, and Mary there were no witnesses—or at least none who wished to come forward.

Sean had spoken with Father Joe again to determine when and where Al's memorial would take place. He assured the priest that he would attend but in plain clothes. He explained that oftentimes killers return to the crime scene or any service for the deceased. Father Joe had cautioned that the church would probably be filled to capacity, making it difficult to see everyone. Sean would be looking for a tall, heavy-set man with bushy hair, who would probably be alone. He knew it was a long shot, but he felt he needed to be there. Following the memorial Mass, the ladies' groups of the parish were having a small reception in the school gym. Sean would be there also.

He also had asked Father Joe if he had any new information, which he didn't. Sean had no way of knowing about Kate's meeting with Father Joe earlier.

Sean had scheduled a meeting first thing Friday morning. All who were working on Al's or Nellie's case would be in attendance. They would rehash all their information on the cases, and Sean would bring up Roger's involvement. Sean would tell them that he planned on talking with Roger over the weekend and, based on their conversation, would let them know the next step. He was sure Roger would be at the hospital over the weekend. Sean wondered if he would attend the memorial Mass.

He put the cases he was working on in separate piles on his desk. Leaving to meet his friend Ernie at a lobster place down the road, Sean planned on trying to forget about his job. *Yeah, right!*

When Kate came in from her visit with Nellie, she prepared her supper, changed into some comfortable clothes, put on her teakettle, and flicked on her TV for the 7:00 news. A policeman was being interviewed by a local news reporter. Kate could tell the interview was taking place in the school parking lot. Evidently a door-to-door canvas had turned up no new clues to Al's murder. Kate switched channels, hoping to catch the weather report, which she did—showers overnight but nice weather through Sunday.

As Kate ate, she read her newspaper. She discovered that an elderly neighbor who had been in a nursing home had passed away. *Nellie knew her too*, thought Kate. She would dig out a Mass card to send to her family. After eating and cleaning up her kitchen, she went hunting for an appropriate card. Finding one, she wrote a consoling note and addressed it.

The telephone rang. It was Andy checking in to see how she was doing. Knowing his mother well, he was sure that underlying her composed exterior were tears just waiting to happen. He had his dad's sensitivity and thoughtfulness ingrained in his very being. He told her about his day, a day in which he had been offered a promotion at his job. It might mean more traveling, but the position would be more rewarding also. Kate could hear the excitement in his voice and congratulated him.

After their conversation, Kate, realizing the hour, got ready for bed. She tossed and turned, unable to get to sleep. When she did doze off, it wasn't for long. Dreams came and went, none of them pleasant, waking her over and over. They contained bits and pieces of unhappy events from the last six months.

CHAPTER 9

Friday, June 21, 2003

At three o'clock a.m., Kate got up and heated some milk. She sat in her darkened kitchen, sipping her milk and wondering what it all meant.

Somewhat relaxed, she went back to bed. This time she slept until six and was awoken by another disturbing dream. In it, she opened the doors to her shed and found a bear cub rifling through a bag of soil. It growled at her and as she stepped back it ran out past her and into the woods.

The first light of the sun was concealed by fog. The overnight rain had ended, leaving beads of moisture on everything. A spider web of indescribable beauty stretched between the rungs of the railing on Kate's porch. She sat at her table, drinking her first cup of coffee and watching the spider work her ways.

Sean Burke was seated at his kitchen counter, also drinking his first cup of coffee for the day. He was planning his day, which included meeting with Kate. All that was left for him was to make a call to her. How to approach his concern, that she had held back information at their last meeting, was on his mind. Also, and perhaps startling to Sean, was how much he was looking forward to seeing her again. She was definitely an attractive woman, but one still grieving the loss of her husband. He refocused his thoughts. *Is there a connection between those three violent acts? And if so, could more violence happen? Who might be next and why?*

He gathered up his breakfast dishes and put them in the sink. Grabbing his keys off the counter, he headed out the door en route to his meeting at the station. He would call Kate after his meeting. Hopefully she would be at home.

The meeting at the police station went pretty much as expected. The only new wrinkle was that the piece of fabric found on Nellie's door jam had been tested and entered as evidence in her case. No DNA had been identified, so in that respect, there were no leads. But it had been determined that the fabric was probably part of a flannel shirt and probably had not been there for a long period of time.

Sean, who believed that good, hard police work found answers, decided to have the investigators of Al's murder go back again and interview not only the school employees but the neighbors as well. He told them he would talk to Father Joe and Kate himself and that all interviews could wait until after the memorial Mass. Before the meeting ended, he had enlisted six officers besides himself and Gerald to attend the service. They all knew what to look for and that it was indeed a long shot.

Kate was vacuuming when her phone rang and she almost didn't hear it, answering on the last ring. Sean quickly apologized for taking her away from whatever she was doing and asked if she would have time to talk to him today. She said she would be home most of the day and invited him to lunch. He was pleasantly surprised and gladly accepted.

After hanging up, Kate put on some potatoes to cook for potato salad and then finished her vacuuming and dusting. When the potatoes were done and cooling, she began putting together a tuna salad, a tossed salad, and a bowl of cut-up fruit. Then she made her potato salad.

The day had become sunny, clear, and almost windless. The table on the porch would be perfect for lunch. As she set the table, Sean's purpose for coming unknown, Kate decided to share her observations of Roger with him. Her talk with Father Joe had steered her in that direction.

At five minutes to one, Kate heard the driveway sensor beep and went out on her porch to meet Sean. Kate noticed that although he was dressed in his uniform, he had driven a regular car and not a cruiser. He did have a small notebook, however, so she knew he was on business. Then he reached back in his car and pulled out a small hanging plant. "Oh, they're lovely, Sergeant!" Kate exclaimed as he handed her the basket of multicolored pansies. "I just love pansies. How kind of you to bring them!"

"I felt I needed to make up for intruding in your life so often, Mrs. Shaw. That and the fact you might need some cheering up after all that's happened," said Sean somewhat awkwardly.

Kate immediately hung the plant on a hook on the porch overhang, thanked him again for being so thoughtful, and invited Sean to take a seat, which he did. She asked him what he would like to drink and went in to get both of them a glass of iced tea. Then she went back in to get all of her salads.

"This looks like a feast fit for a king," said Sean appreciatively. "It's certainly not my regular lunch on the run." They ate slowly, making small talk about Kate's yard and the view from the porch. He shared with her the progress, or lack of it, on both Nellie's and Al's cases.

"I'm not surprised that there were no witnesses to Al's murder," Kate said slowly. "Everyone pretty much clears out quickly on the last day of school. The only reason I was still there was because it was my last day and I was trying to pack up some things to take home. I imagine that you questioned the neighbors," she asked, assuming the answer.

"Without any luck, I'm afraid," said Sean. "Many hadn't gotten home from work at that time, and those that were home were either unable or unwilling to help."

Kate sat quietly, somewhat deep in thought. "You know, Sergeant," she said, "I wonder if you might have missed someone. The high school kids in the neighborhood get out quite a bit earlier than we do, and sometimes they come to the parking lot to ride their skateboards. I can't say that I saw any that day, but that doesn't mean one of them wasn't around."

"That's a real possibility, Mrs. Shaw. I'll have someone stake out the parking lot. Maybe we'll get lucky. Teens tend not to be very easy to question at times," he added.

"Was there anything new that you wanted to tell me, Mrs. Shaw?" he asked.

Kate swallowed hard and told him about Roger's unusual behavior and how she felt about sharing that information with him.

He listened quietly, aware that his initial feelings about her holding back were correct but understanding why she did so. "I appreciate your reluctance to share this with me even now, Mrs. Shaw," said Sean. "I know how close you are to Mrs. Stevens and her sons. Let's not assume anything here. I plan on speaking with both of her sons. Now that she is improving, perhaps Roger will volunteer the fact that he was over his mother's house and why without my asking. I'm sure both of them know that we are now treating her fall as a possible home invasion. I had planned to speak with her when she was up to it, too." He gave her the key to Nellie's house that Bob had given him.

Kate smiled gratefully. She had been right about trusting Sean.

Sean helped Kate clear the table despite her protests. That done, he told her that he would probably see her at the memorial Mass, and they said their good-byes.

Soon after Sean left, Elizabeth called to ask how she was. She also wanted to know if she should wear black to the memorial Mass.

"Black is not necessary, Elizabeth," Kate told her. "I'm wearing my tan pantsuit."

They finished their conversation and Kate left to visit Nellie at the hospital—after she stopped to pick up some flowers.

When Kate entered Nellie's room, she was surprised to see both Bob and Roger. Nellie was once again out to physical therapy. Kate was struck by how much better Roger looked. They exchanged their hellos, and after both boys planted kisses on her cheek, she set about looking for a vase for the flowers. Finding none, she headed out to the nurses' station. As she returned with a vase, she could hear Roger's animated voice telling Bob about his new job. Kate couldn't help but think that things would work out. No sooner had she had the flowers set, Nellie was brought back in. Seeing the three of them, she beamed. The nurse left her in her wheelchair.

Roger quickly told his mother how his new boss had come to him and asked about her and told him to leave early to see her. Then he told Nellie and Kate about his job. Nellie agreed that it sounded like a good fit for him. The fact that his office was only a twenty-minute ride from his condo was an added plus.

As they were visiting, the hospital social worker came in to discuss Nellie's move to a nursing home. Kate could tell that the boys weren't too happy about it, but Nellie took it in stride. Dr. Moore had discussed with Nellie the fact that she would need specialized help for at least a month. After that, they could see whether she could go home with part-time help. Kate thought to herself that when that time came, she would offer to have Nellie come home to her house for as long as needed, but she would talk to the boys alone about that possibility before saying anything to Nellie.

The social worker told them that Nellie would be ready for the move on Tuesday. The nursing home would be much closer to Nellie's house, so it would be easier for Kate and Bob to get there.

After the social worker left, a nurse came in to check on Nellie and bring her supper. Kate could see that Nellie was tired but encouraged her to eat as much as she could before getting back in bed.

Both Bob and Roger would be staying at Nellie's house over the weekend, with Roger returning to his condo Sunday night. Bob would be going back home and to his job after Nellie was settled in the nursing home. Kate invited them both for supper Sunday, thinking they must be tired of hospital food, but they declined. Kate, thinking that they'd want to spend the time with Nellie, didn't remind them about Al's memorial Mass the next day. After Nellie was helped into bed, Kate told her she was going to go home. She gave Bob the key that Sergeant Burke had given her.

During the drive home, Kate thought about the day's happenings. She would finish up the leftovers from lunch for supper, along with a cup of tea.

After supper, Kate cleaned up the dishes and her kitchen. Then she went into the den and turned on the news. The news team was seated at their desk and behind them was a smiling picture of Al. The story was about Al and the fact that there would be a memorial Mass the next day at Sacred Heart. It hurt to hear about Al's contributions to the community, especially to the school, and his senseless murder. Kate found herself crying. She turned off the news, determined that the TV would not go on again anytime soon.

An hour later, Kate climbed into bed. She lay there thinking about the day ahead and hoping all would go well. She soon went into an untroubled sleep.

Sean was also preparing to go to bed. He had showered and shaved, hoping to be able to get an early start in the morning. The thought crossed his mind that he wasn't sure what the memorial Mass would be like the next day. He had been estranged from the church since the death of his wife three years earlier.

At first it was his anger at God that kept him away. After that, it was his embarrassment over being away so long. As he climbed into bed, he decided he would talk to Father Joe about it when he went to interview him again. He felt that Father Joe was the right person to help him find his way back. He would sleep well tonight.

Across town, a troubled soul sat in the dark in a small three-room apartment. In his lap was the outfit he would wear to the memorial Mass. His grim features displayed no remorse. In this outfit, he wouldn't have to show sadness, only resignation and faith. He could pull it off. He would rise early and give himself a close shave. His head was already bald, the wig he had worn only last week stored carefully away.

Yes, he would have to endure the accolades for Al Watson, but seeing others grieving, especially Kate Shaw, would more than offset that.

His churning anger wouldn't let him sleep this night.

CHAPTER 10

Saturday, June 22, 2003

The ringing phone woke Kate from a sound sleep. She could tell it was still dark out as she reached for the phone. As she answered it, she glanced at the clock next to her bed. Four-thirty. Again, there was no one on the other end. All the worried thoughts that go through a mother's mind and shake her to the core caused Kate to shiver. A mixture of anger and relief coursed through her. She got up and went to the bathroom. She climbed back into bed. *Maybe if I lay here awhile, I can get back to sleep.* She thought about the upcoming Mass and about the last day she saw Al. Only good thoughts came to her. She knew the memorial Mass would do Al justice. The music and readings were ones he would have chosen. She rolled over on her side and, remarkably, dozed off. Too soon her alarm went off.

After her usual walk and pickup of her newspaper, Kate put on the coffee and went to take a shower. By seven-thirty she was dressed and sitting at her kitchen table, reading the paper as she ate. On the first page of the town section was a picture of Al with an accompanying article. It was well written and emphasized Al's life and community contributions, rather than his untimely death, although there was the mention of the killer still being at large. Once again Kate was forced to think about that last day. *Who could have done this and why? Will we ever know?*

By the time she finished her breakfast and cleared the table, Kate had answered three phone calls—one from each of her boys and one from Jan. She cleaned up her kitchen and went to get her purse and pantsuit jacket from her closet. She would be ready to go when her family came for her.

Sean arrived at Sacred Heart right after the seven-thirty Mass. He found Father Joe in the Sacristy. "Hello Father, how are you today?" he asked.

"I'm all right under the circumstances, Sergeant Burke, and you?" Father Joe replied.

Sean realized that Al's death had had a profound effect on Father Joe. *We think of priests being somehow insulated from loss, exempt from grief,* thought Sean. He told the priest that he and his officers would be placing cameras at the church entrances and in the flower arrangements in an attempt to have photos of those in attendance. He would position the six other officers, who were in plain clothes, as he was, around the church.

Father Joe nodded. He then told Sean that Al's nephew from Minnesota would be sitting in the second row on the left with the faculty families. On one hand, he was not happy with what the police wanted to do, but on the other, he understood the need.

The other officers would arrive at staggered times, infiltrating themselves throughout the congregation. Two of them would come in as a couple. Gerald would be in the choir loft. A practicing Catholic, he would be more apt to see any unusual behavior, such as someone not genuflecting or the like but would keep in mind that non-Catholics would be attending. Of course, if the killer were Catholic, he could go undetected.

Sacred Heart was built a century earlier, in the shape of a cross with a center aisle and two side aisles, one on each side of the church. Beautiful stained-glass windows lined the outside walls. All were donated by members of the parish when it was built or by priests who had served there at the time. Sean took his seat in the east wing of the church. He would be able to see those on the altar and those doing readings, as well as that side of the church.

As he sat there, he thought of the last time he was there. It was at the funeral of his wife, Rita. She had fought a three-year battle with cancer, to no avail. Sean had watched her, a vibrant woman full of hope, weighing one hundred thirty pounds, become a weak invalid of ninety pounds. She never lost her faith in God or that she would beat the odds. But he had. Grief, loss, anger, and hopelessness had combined to turn him against his God. She had been his life. Without her, he only had his job.

Flower baskets were in front of the altar, the lectern, and the statues of St. Joseph and the Blessed Virgin Mary. The large green basket in front of the altar held red and white flowers—the school's colors. The others contained various spring flowers. The first four rows on each side of the center aisle were reserved. *Probably for the faculty and their families*, thought Sean.

At about nine o'clock, the organist, Mrs. Thompson, came in and went up to the choir loft. Soon she was softly playing the songs that would be used at the Mass. Sean marveled at the wonderful acoustics of the church and how beautifully she played. He turned and looked up at the choir loft. He didn't remember ever seeing the intricate sculptured railing. While he was looking up, he saw Gerald take his place.

After kneeling for a short time, Gerald sat back. He had a wonderful view, except for the area under the choir loft. Not only would he be able to see people entering from all sides, but more importantly, because he could see their faces, he would see them leaving. As he sat there listening to the softly played music, he heard footsteps on the stairs to the choir loft.

Entering and sitting to his left were the members of the parish choir. They were an assortment of middle-aged and older, tall and short, men and women. From what he could tell, most were probably retired. They quietly visited among themselves until the organist passed out the program of songs for them to look over. Then Mrs. Thompson came over to him and gave him a complete program of the Mass. She explained that all the members but one had been members for a number of years and could sing a cappella. The newer member was a woman. No one in the group resembled the suspect. He assured Mrs. Thompson that from what he had heard, her playing was wonderful. Mrs. Thompson thanked him and began putting copies of the songs on the pews behind him. He wondered why she was doing that because the loft was usually the last place people would sit at a memorial.

It wasn't long before he had his answer. Schoolchildren were joining him. After genuflecting, they took their places in the pews on his side of the organ. The girls wore their plaid jumpers and white blouses; the boys wore dark blue pants, light blue shirts, and plaid ties, which matched the girls' jumpers. Two women, who were probably their teachers, followed them in. One sat in back of them and the other took her place on a folding chair behind a music stand next to the railing.

Memories of his own days at Sacred Heart flooded over Gerald. True, it was different now. There were no teaching nuns any longer. The classes were smaller than when he attended, but the sense of family lingered. The children, of what he thought ranged in ages from eight to thirteen, grades three to eight, were interspersed. In his day, the classes would be separate, the youngest toward the front, the older children in the back, boys on one side of the organ, girls on the other, the numbers much larger. But then as now, he reflected, the raised steps in the loft allowed everyone to see over the railing. He wondered who had called their parents to summon them.

He looked down and saw people straggling into the church. The first rows on either side of the main aisle were filling up rapidly with teachers and their families, except for the first and second rows on the left. Those were left empty for those who would be doing the readings and their families.

Father Joe, already dressed in his vestments, came out and walked to the lectern, where he inspected the folder that held the readings. Then he put a small communion box on the altar for one of the Eucharistic ministers who would visit a sick person after the Mass. Back in the Sacristy, he readied the water and wine, which was to be used at Mass, as well as the communion wafers. Two of the eighth grade students who would serve as altar servers took the cruets and wafer bowl, or Paten, and carried them down to the cross section of the center aisle, placing them on the shelf in front of two students who had graduated in June.

They would bring the water, wine, and the Paten with the communion wafers up to the altar at Offertory time.

The organist began to play quietly.

Sean noticed that Kate's family and Jan and her husband had entered and seated themselves in the second row on the left. *Kate is probably doing one of the readings.* Behind them were three nuns who took seats in the row behind the reserved rows on the left. He was surprised at seeing nuns, as he knew there were none teaching at the school. He noticed that although they all wore black and white habits, the styles of them were somewhat different. The first nun had a veil that covered her ears, but her hair could be seen sticking out and her habit ended mid calf. The second had small veil and a turtleneck sweater under her habit, which was ankle length. The third nun was dressed in what he considered a "severe" veil and habit, where you could only see her face and hands.

He recalled that after the 1960s, many nuns wore regular clothes as they became less cloistered and more involved in the public domain. Then he remembered that there was a small community who lived in the next town and ministered primarily to the poor by making and selling bread.

Andy sat listening to the music, thinking back to not so long ago, when he was at his beloved Molly's funeral Mass. His parents had thought they were too young to take on the responsibilities of marriage, but they were supportive none the less, accepting Molly as the daughter they never had. Her parents, too, treated him like a son.

The pain and feelings of loss were still there. It would be two years in January since she was struck down by a hit-and-run driver whom the police had never found. He knew his whole family missed her wonderful spirit, so warm and giving. He doubted there would ever be another for him.

The church bells tolled solemnly in the steeple, calling the congregation to enter the church. The door to the Sacristy opened, and out came Father Joe, who walked to the back of the church, followed by Kate, the three altar servers who were carrying the candles and crucifix, and the student who carried the school banner. The church continued to fill up as the ten o'clock hour approached.

Gerald had also watched the arrival of Kate's family and other teachers and the procession of servers, Father Joe, and Kate, as they went to the back of the church. Four adults followed, but went to sit in the right front pew. They would help distribute Holy Communion later. Scanning the church, he saw his fellow police officers in place, with the exception of one who probably was out of sight at the back of the church. So far, he had seen no one and nothing out of the ordinary.

The church continued to fill to capacity. Gerald and Sean could see many clutching tissues and trying to put forward brave faces.

A young child, probably ten years old, left the pew where he had been sitting with his family and went toward the altar. When he reached the step, he bowed slightly and proceeded to the lectern. For a moment he could not be seen as he was placing a small stool in place so he could stand on it to reach the microphone.

Suddenly, outside the church a loud siren blared, disrupting the quietness of the moment and the thoughts of many. Startled, all looked to the windows on the side of the church where the sound was coming from and murmured to those next to them. School children blessed themselves and said a prayer for whoever was in need.

He was sure he had been discovered and raised his handkerchief to his face to wipe away perspiration on his forehead. He looked slowly to his left toward the siren. *I should have brought my gun and ended it all now.*

Two men, one on either side of the church, jumped to their feet, climbed over people in their row, and ran for the exit.

The initial siren of the fire engine was joined by the two other sirens on the cars of the volunteer firemen who, minutes ago, had left the church. Slowly all three sirens faded into the distance. The congregation let out a collective sigh of relief and once again looked toward the front of the church.

John Logan stood at the lectern for a moment while the congregation settled down. All eyes were on this tow-headed young boy dressed in the school uniform. He glanced at a young woman, probably his mother, and then looked out into the church. He began: "Good Morning. We are here today to celebrate the life of our principal, Mr. Alfred Watson, and to pray for the repose of his soul. I am John Logan. Our readers today will be Mrs. Kate Shaw, Melanie Rogers, and Thomas King. Our gift bearers are alumni students Susan Campbell and Jose Constantine. Our altar servers are Mary DeRoss, Collin Walsh, and Maurice Flanagan. Luke Engler will carry in our school banner. Father Joe will be our celebrant. Our opening hymn is 'On Eagles

Wings,' number 168 in the hymnal. Please stand and raise your voices."

As the organist began playing, John left the lectern, walked down in front of the altar, bowed, and went to stand with his parents. All in the church stood.

Leading the procession was Collin Walsh, holding the crucifix. He was followed by the other two altar servers who were carrying candles and behind them, carrying the school banner, was Luke Engler. Behind them were the two youngsters who would be doing readings, and behind them, Kate, who was holding a large book of gospels above her head. Father Joe followed her.

All bowed as they reached the altar, the altar servers going up to the altar, Luke Engler placing the school banner in its stand to the right of the altar and sitting to the side, and the two readers going into the left front pew. Kate went up to the altar and placed the book standing open on the altar, bowed, and went to stand in the pew with the other readers. Father Joe took his place behind the altar, facing the congregation.

Sean was amazed at the precision of the youngsters who were participating in the Mass. He had never been to a Mass where the children had been allowed to be readers. He was also impressed by the opening song that was chosen. *How comforting*, he thought.

Elsewhere, another stood, trying to keep his emotions under control, thinking to himself that Al didn't deserve to have the children involved in the Mass. His hymnal open, he only mouthed the words.

Father Joe began the opening prayer, which included the sign of the cross. After that, all were seated to hear the readings.

Kate approached the altar, bowed, and went to the lectern. The reading that she and Father Joe had chosen came from the book of Wisdom.

It spoke about just men: She said, "A reading from the book of Wisdom."

> But the souls of the just are in the hand of God,
> And no torment shall touch them.
> They seemed, in the view of the foolish,
> To be dead;
> And their passing away was thought an affliction,
> And their going forth from us, utter destruction.
> But they are in peace.
> For if before men, indeed, they be punished,
> Yet is their hope full of immortality;
> Chastised a little, they shall be greatly blessed,
> Because God tried them
> And found them worthy of Himself.
>
> Wisdom 3:1–5 (NAB)

"The Word of the Lord"

He wasn't just or fair. He was deceitful, pretending to be helping me when behind my back destroying my family, and she's no better. He felt the bile rising in his throat. He took out his handkerchief and covered his mouth.

Finished with the reading, Kate walked to the front of the altar, where she met the next reader, Melanie Rodgers. They bowed together, Kate went back to her seat, and Melanie went up to the lectern. Melanie bent down and placed the stool in place so that she could reach. She said, "Please respond" and the well-known words, "The Lord is my Shepherd, there is nothing I shall want."

Those in attendance echoed the response. She continued with the psalm, each time ending with the response, which the congregation repeated. Finished, she too left the lectern and met the next reader, Thomas King, in front of the altar.

Thomas moved the stool because he could reach without it. Then he looked out into the waiting faces and cleared his throat and took a deep breath.

He, above all the other students, was especially close to Al. His father had died when he was only four and his mother tried to be both mother and father. As he reached the upper grades, she was unable to help him with his homework in science and math. Her strong suit was liberal arts, especially English grammar and literature. Al tutored him after school three days a week. An intelligent boy, he gradually improved his grades in his weak subjects. He would proudly bring his math tests to Al and his mother to see.

He and Al also shared an interest in sports. Al had encouraged him to go out for basketball and made it a point to go to his games. He knew now he would have to once again "go it alone" with just his mother.

In a clear voice he said, "A reading from the letter of St. Paul to the Colossians":

Because you are God's chosen ones, holy and beloved,
Clothe yourselves with heartfelt mercy, with kindness,
Humility, meekness, and patience.
Bear with one another; forgive whatever grievances
You have against one another.
Forgive as the Lord has forgiven you.
Over all these virtues put on love,
Which binds the rest together and makes them perfect.
Christ's peace must reign in your hearts,
Since as members of the one body you have
Been called to that peace.
Dedicate yourselves to thankfulness.
Let the word of Christ, rich as it is, dwell in you.
In wisdom made perfect, instruct and
Admonish one another.
Sing gratefully to God from your hearts in psalms,
Hymns, and inspired songs.
Whatever you do, whether in speech or in action,
Do it in the name of the Lord Jesus.
Give thanks to God the Father through him.

Colossians 3:12–16 (NAB)

"The Word of the Lord."

As Thomas said these final words, tears were streaming down his cheeks. He looked over at Father Joe, who nodded and smiled. Thomas, as had the others, walked to the front of the altar, bowed, and returned to his seat. He sat next to Kate, who put her arm around his shoulder.

Then an angelic young voice came from the choir loft. A young girl had come forward from her seat to the railing of the choir loft and begun to sing the Alleluia refrain to announce the gospel reading. Standing, the congregation repeated the three alleluias, and she sang the verse. Her beautiful voice projected out into the whole church, hushing its occupants.

Gerald watched her closely. He figured she must be an eighth grader. *But with so much poise,* he thought. He looked past her to the standing assembly.

Father Joe took the book from the altar and walked to the lectern. He announced, "The gospel according to John":

> "Do not let your hearts be troubled.
> Have faith in God;
> and faith in me.
> In my Father's house there are many dwelling places;
> otherwise, how could I have told you
> that I was going to prepare a place for you?
> I am indeed going to prepare a place for you,
> and then I shall come back to take you with me,
> that where I am you also may be.
> You know the way that leads where I go."
> 'Lord,' said Thomas, 'we do not know where you are going.
> How can we know the way?'
> Jesus told him, 'I am the way and the truth, and the life;
> no one comes to the Father but through me.'"
>
> John 14:1–6 (NAB)

"The Word of the Lord."

After acknowledging those present, including Jeffrey Watson, Al's nephew, Father Joe began his homily:

"In these readings today there is a common theme of justice, love, faith, and trust between God the Father, Jesus, and humanity. My friend, Al Watson, was a just man. He had a deep faith in his God and a love for not just his God, but also those around him. He demonstrated all this day after day as he administered Sacred Heart School. We all trusted him. He believed he had a mission here—that he was doing what Jesus wanted him to do. That he leaves a void in our lives and our hearts have no doubt. But keep in mind, though you grieve, that a place prepared for him in heaven has surely been filled. Where does that leave us? To follow his example: to be just, to believe, to love, and to trust that we will one day see him again when we take our prepared places. God bless you all."

There was not a dry eye in the church but one.

Father Joe went back up to his seat behind the altar and sat for a few minutes with head bowed. All that could be heard was the swishing of the ceiling fans.

Then a muffled thud came from somewhere just in front of where the gift bearers sat, unnerving many. Almost every head turned in that direction. Quickly, Gerald went to the railing to look down. A small boy, maybe four years old, was down on his knees in the pew retrieving the missal he had dropped.

Relieved, all turned to face front again.

When Father Joe stood, all stood to take part in the recitation of the Nicene Creed, which states what Catholics believe.

One nun, handkerchief partially covering her face, quietly left her pew and slowly walked toward the side entrance where the bathroom was located. Gerald watched her go through the double doors and then looked back toward the altar in prayer.

In the small bathroom, he wretched. Then he angrily stripped off his habit and veil. *Fools, they wouldn't know a corrupt man if they saw one.* He lowered his pant legs, which had been tied around his knees with twine. He rolled the habit and veil into a ball and, putting it under his arm, he left the bathroom and went out the side door. Taking long strides, he crossed the street to the parking lot of a small market and got in his car. He was careful to pull slowly out of the lot and drive off so as not to attract attention.

Inside the church, Kate was finishing up the petitions, which included prayers for Al and various other intentions. As she made her way back to her seat, the altar servers readied the altar for the Consecration of the gifts. Father Joe sat quietly, head bowed, meditating. The organist began playing "Amazing Grace," and the altar servers retrieved the candles and cross and went down the aisle to escort the gift bearers—Susan Campbell and Jose Constantine. She, with tears steaming down her face, and he, stoically looking straight ahead, followed the altar servers with the communion hosts and the water and wine cruets to a waiting Father Joe, who had come to the altar's edge to meet them. Father Joe took the cruets and host bowl and gave them to the altar servers to place on the altar then embraced both young people. They then bowed toward the altar and returned to their seats.

All in the church sat quietly, many reflecting on their own personal memories of Al and, surely, other lost loved ones.

Gerald, realizing that the nun had not returned, left his seat in the choir loft and went down to the floor below on his way to the bathroom. He found the door ajar and no occupant. He quickly went outdoors but found no one there either. He came back in, heading for the choir loft, and took his seat again. Either the nun had taken ill and left, or someone dressed as a nun couldn't finish out the Mass. He would know that answer when he spoke with the remaining nuns after Mass.

Being on the other side of the church, Sean hadn't noticed the nun in question leaving her seat, but during the Consecration he did notice that there were only two seated there. He turned to give his full attention to Father Joe on the altar, when he heard the Consecration bells ring. He was surprised how much he had missed this. A longing to receive Communion overtook him, but he decided he needed to go to confession first, so he just prayed for help with his return.

The Eucharistic ministers went up on the altar to receive and get individual bowls of Communion hosts to distribute to the congregation. One of them left the altar and proceeded up to the choir loft to give Communion to those there. Father Joe stood in front of the altar, and the other Eucharistic ministers went to the side aisles. The organist played the hymn "Take this Bread" as the faithful left their pews and went forward to receive. Many asked for a blessing instead of receiving. Sean was one of those.

As the end of the line drew near, the schoolchildren around Gerald in the choir loft stood and began to sing a song called "Hail Mary, Gentle Woman." The sound of the pure voices and how they shadowed different parts of the song caused some to turn and look up at them.

Father Joe was back on the altar purifying the chalice and other containers that had held the Hosts. He returned the unused Hosts to the tabernacle at the side altar and took his seat behind the altar.

Those who had been kneeling in prayer sat also. Then the students in the choir loft sang the "Ave Maria" in Latin. They sounded like angels, and tears flowed anew.

Even Father Joe's eyes filled. He had lost a good friend to violence, right in the school they both loved so dearly. He thought about his impending trip to Minnesota with Jeffrey Watson that afternoon. He would say the funeral Mass for Al the following Monday. He would meet Al's relatives, answer questions, and try to console.

The song ended, and Father Joe rose and told everyone that there would be some comments to follow.

Slowly, once again Thomas King approached the altar, bowed, and went up to the lectern. This time he took out a folded piece of paper and laid it flat. He began by thanking everyone for coming and then began to tell what Al meant to him and other students. His voice was steady. This was his gift to Al. He would not cry; those tears had already been shed. The time was for memories, especially in the area of sports.

Next came Kate. She also shared memories. She talked about Al's interaction with the faculty and staff, how approachable and understanding Al was, and how he worked to make Sacred Heart a perfect place to be for others, whether child or adult.

Lastly Al's nephew, Jeffrey, went up to the lectern. He also thanked everyone for coming. Father Joe was thanked for not only the beautiful Mass which he had said that day, but for returning with him to Minnesota to say Al's funeral Mass. Then he spoke about how Al and his aunt Rita were there for him when he lost his father and how Al was like a second father to him when he was growing up.

After Jeffrey returned to his seat, Father Joe stood, told everyone that they were welcome in the gym to take part in the reception that the two ladies' organizations had prepared, and then asked people to stand for the final blessing.

The cross bearer and candleholders, followed by the school banner bearer, led the procession out. Father Joe walked behind them. The schoolchildren and the parish choir sang "How Great Thou Art" as a closing song. Once again the steeple bells rang, this time signaling the end of the Mass.

Gerald, wanting to be sure to talk to the nuns, left his seat and headed downstairs before the song was finished. He was successful in reaching them before they left the church. As he had suspected, the nun who had left early was unknown to them, having simply followed them in to their seats.

Sean came over to him, and Gerald told him what he had seen. They inspected the pew and the bathroom, hoping to find something left behind, but there was nothing.

The other officers had gone with everyone else over to the hall where the reception was being held. They would go back later and retrieve the cameras. Sean and Gerald sat in a pew and discussed what had transpired. "I guess we'll have to look at whatever was caught on the video cameras, Gerald," said Sean.

"We do stand a pretty good chance of getting a look at him on either the altar one or the one outside the side door, Sergeant," said Gerald.

"Let's go over to the hall," said Sean. Gerald nodded, and they quietly left the church.

As they entered the hall, Sean and Gerald could see Father Joe, Kate, her family, and Jeffrey Watson standing together talking. Rather then joining them, they separated and walked around, watching for anyone who was alone. There were many small groups, and they heard over and over again favorable comments about the Mass and also comments about Al. Everyone's mood was subdued.

The ladies' organizations had set up three tables, and all were filled with an assortment of foods: small sandwiches, punch, fruit salads, Jell-O salads, and desserts. Against one wall were coffee urns, milk, sugar, and juice, along with paper cups and stirrers.

Sean went over there to get a cup of coffee. At the same time Michael Shaw came over. They were out of everyone's hearing for the moment.

"Sergeant, do you think my mother is in any danger?" Michael asked.

"Why do you ask?"

"Well, I know you have been to see her a couple of times, and my wife tells me that my mother has been getting hang up calls," Michael said.

"I didn't know about those calls, Michael, but I am concerned that she has lost people close to her and had one close friend seriously injured recently. What I'm trying to determine is whether there is a connection with your father's death, Al Watson's death, and Mrs. Stevens's accident," said Sean quietly.

Michael paled. "Please keep me informed, Sergeant. I won't say anything to my mother because I don't want to worry her," he said quietly. "But I will keep closer tabs on her."

"I think that is the best way to handle it, Michael," said Sean. At that point Michael went back to where Kate was, and Sean went to look for Gerald.

Little by little, the hall emptied out, eventually leaving Sean, Gerald, Father Joe, Jeffrey Watson, Kate, her family, and the ladies who were cleaning up. In answer to Jeffrey's question, Sean told them what had been done so far in the investigation and where it would go next. He didn't mention the "nun" but did tell them about the cameras, which were, at that moment, being retrieved from the church. Jeffrey thanked him for all that he was doing to solve the case.

Then, telling them that he and Jeffrey had to get ready for the afternoon flight to Minnesota, Father Joe and Jeffrey left for the rectory.

Sean and Gerald also excused themselves and left.

Kate went over to the women who had prepared the reception, told them how delicious everything was, and thanked them. Then she joined Andrew, Michael, and Elizabeth, and they left the hall. They had all come from her house in one car, so they returned there.

They were all ready for a cool drink and some cookies, and they sat out on Kate's front porch at the table. Michael asked her about Nellie, and she told him that Nellie had improved to the point that she would be going to a nursing home sometime next week. There she would continue her physical therapy. The plan was for her to come home to Kate's house when she was more mobile. Kate added, before they had a chance to ask, that Nellie still didn't remember what had happened to her. She also told them that she planned on going in to see her later on.

After Andrew, Elizabeth, and Michael left, Kate changed clothes and headed out for the hospital. There she had a chance to talk to both Bob and Roger, as Nellie was once again at a therapy session.

She told them all about Al's Mass. They told her that Nellie would be going to the nursing home on Monday. She assured them that she would visit her every day and feed Samantha. Roger's new job continued to go well; Bob had used up his vacation time, so he needed to be back on Tuesday. Bob told her he would drop off the key to Nellie's house when he was ready to leave.

After Nellie had eaten her supper and was dozing, the three of them decided to go out to eat.

Kate was grateful because she didn't really feel like being alone that night. They went to the diner that Kate and Bob had been to before and had a very good meal. Both Bob and Roger would be staying at Nellie's house over the weekend. Kate asked if they would like to come for supper at her house Sunday night. They said they would see how things went with their mother and would let her know mid-day. They left the diner together, all heading for the parking lot. They got in their separate cars and headed home—Kate to her house and the Stevens boys to Nellie's house.

It was almost nine o'clock when Kate entered her kitchen. Although tired, she put on her teapot for a cup of tea. Then she went into her bedroom and got ready for bed.

She sat at her kitchen table, slowly sipping her tea and thinking about Al's Mass.

By ten she was in bed, watching the late news. There was a short story on Al's funeral. After hearing the weather, Kate turned off her lamp by the bed and went to sleep.

CHAPTER 11

Sunday, June 23, 2003

Sunday arrived very differently than Saturday. Rather than bright sunshine, it was overcast to the point of feeling like impending rain.

Kate did her usual walk and paper pickup. Inside, she set up her coffee pot and went in for her shower. She had decided to go to the nine o'clock Mass. Jan had invited her for lunch, so she would go over her house after a stop at the supermarket, where she would pick up some flowers.

Jan was sitting out on her porch when Kate arrived. She, of course, loved the flowers and gave Kate a hug as she took them from her. Jan's husband, Scott, came up from his garden and gave her a hug also.

"No rest for the weary, Scott?" Kate kidded.

"Well, someone has to plant the garden," he replied, looking past her at his wife.

Then the conversation turned to a more subdued tone, with Scott telling Kate what a lovely Mass it was the day before. Kate agreed that the children had done an exceptional job, as had the ladies' organizations. None of them were surprised by the turnout.

Scott went inside to clean up, and Jan and Kate sat on the porch. Jan asked Kate what she thought Father Joe would do about a replacement for Al. "I really don't know, Jan," Kate said. "At least he has the summer to look for one. I think when he gets back home, he might call a meeting of the faculty to see if anyone has anyone in mind. It won't be easy to find someone of Al's caliber at the pay we can afford."

"He was certainly one of a kind, Kate," Jan said.

Scott rejoined them, and they talked about other things until Jan excused herself to bring out lunch items.

While eating a wonderful lunch, Kate updated them about Nellie. Lunch done, Scott went back to his garden, and Jan and Kate talked about school things, mainly about what Kate still had to do to clean out her room. She told Jan that she probably only needed a couple of days more.

"We certainly have a way of building inventory over a career," said Kate wistfully. Jan agreed and once again offered her help, which Kate refused, saying, "It's pretty much a one-person job." After cleaning up the lunch items, they sat back down with iced teas and made small talk.

Sean was riding an elevator to Nellie's floor. He had spoken with her doctor and had gotten an okay to question her. He thought that both sons would be there, and he would talk to them also.

As Sean exited onto her floor, he turned right. Nellie's room was near the nurses' station. When he entered her room, he found her in a wheelchair talking to her two sons and introduced himself to her. "Mrs. Stevens, Dr. Moore said you might feel up to telling me what you remember about your accident," he began.

Nellie answered that she'd be more than happy to tell him what she remembered, but she felt she wouldn't be much help. Bob and Roger sat nearby.

"I had driven into town to pick up some groceries about three-thirty on Thursday. I remember wanting to get back in time to talk to Kate. She usually gets home by four o'clock, and we have tea together. I hadn't felt well earlier, or I would have gone to the prayer service that they have on the last day. That's all I remember."

"Mom," Bob asked. "Do you remember calling me and canceling your visit that afternoon?"

"No, I don't, dear," said Nellie.

"It is really surprising how much a bump on the head can do to one's memory, Mrs. Stevens," said Sean thoughtfully. "But perhaps after you have a chance to heal a little longer you'll be able to tell me more about your fall." At that, he handed her his card and told her that he would welcome a call from her if she thought of anything else. As he stood, a nurse came in to take Nellie down for therapy.

After she had left, Sean turned to Bob and Roger, who were also standing. "I wonder if I might have a few moments," he said to them.

Sean proceeded to tell them about the piece of flannel shirt the police had found in Nellie's house and where. Both Bob and Roger were surprised, and Roger wondered aloud if his mother had any work done there lately. Bob said none that he knew of.

"Do either of you ever wear flannel shirts?" asked Sean. Both looked at each other and back at Sean, shaking their heads.

Then Roger said, "Sergeant, there is something I should tell you that I didn't mention before. I went to visit Mother around two o'clock on the afternoon of her accident. I came to tell her about my new job and to ask her once again to come and live with me. I told her I would be able to support both of us now. She could sell her house and invest it so she'd have money to spend on whatever she wished. She was thrilled about my new job, but didn't want to even think about selling her house.

"She said that she couldn't leave Mrs. Shaw and her other friends. Plus, she enjoyed helping out at the school. I have to admit I wasn't too happy about it, and I left right away, even though she wanted me to stay for supper. Boy, I wish I had stayed."

Sean could see that this was the first Bob had heard of Roger being at his mother's that fateful day.

"Why didn't you tell us about it, Roger?" his brother asked, visibly shaken. "Mom never mentioned your visit."

"At first I was so worried about Mom, and I blamed myself. If I had stayed, perhaps this wouldn't have happened to her."

"I wish you had mentioned it, Roger," said Sean. "Especially now, since we are handling her fall as other than accidental. At least Bob talked to her later that day so I'm sure that someone saw you back at your home or office, so you're not a suspect. We think her fall came sometime after she spoke to your brother."

"Thank you, Sergeant Burke," said Roger. "I'm sure I can give you the names of some people who I was with."

"Sergeant, although my mother doesn't remember, she did know about Mr. Watson's death, because she told me she was going to stay home because of it," said Bob.

Sean nodded and then said his goodbyes, thanking them for their help.

As he was entering the elevator, Nellie was being wheeled back to her room. He waved, but she didn't seem to remember him and looked away.

When Kate arrived, Roger had already gone home, but Bob told her all about Sean's visit.

"I'm so relieved that there was a logical explanation, Bob," she said and told him about how she had known the direction that the investigation was taking. She also told him how worried she had been about Roger and his attitude.

Bob told her that the next morning would be spent getting Nellie settled in the nursing home, but then he would stop by her house before heading back to his home and job. Once again, Kate told him she would visit Nellie and take care of Samantha during the week. Nellie was wheeled back into her room, and the three had a nice visit. When Nellie dropped off to sleep, Kate gave Bob a hug and headed home.

As Kate drove up her street, she could see a vehicle pulling out of her driveway. She could only see that it was white. She couldn't make out the make, model, or license plate number because it was going in the other direction. *I wonder who that could have been?* She pulled into her garage and went inside her mudroom. She opened her side door to check if a package or note had been left but found none. As she entered her house, the phone was ringing, and she rushed to answer it.

"Kate, it's Margot!"

"Margot," exclaimed Kate. "I'm so glad to hear your voice! How was your trip?"

"I can't wait to tell you all about it, Kate, but first I want to hear all about what you've been going through. I had no idea."

"Don't feel badly about it, Margot. I knew you were out of the country and probably didn't hear about it," said Kate. "Why don't we meet for lunch at my house tomorrow?"

Margot thought that was a wonderful idea, and they set the time at one o'clock. After Kate hung up, she thought to herself that that would give her time to work on her classroom at school and pick up a few things at the grocery store.

Kate found that she had little appetite, so she decided to make a soft-boiled egg on toast and a cup of tea for supper. She set up a TV table in her den and watched the national news while she ate.

After cleaning up the dishes, she got ready for bed and hopped in, intending once again to get into her book. She hadn't read more than four chapters before she dozed off. She awoke in time to watch the late news. Then she went back to bed for the night.

The white car that Kate had seen earlier was parked on another residential street. Its occupant was watching a small ranch house. As he watched, a dark blue car pulled into the driveway, and a woman went into the house. Within minutes, a young girl, probably high school age, left the house and walked down the street away from his car. When she reached a house three doors down, she went in.

Neither the woman in the first house nor the teenager in the next house were aware of his surveillance. After the lights went out at the first house, he drove down the street with his lights off until he reached the stop sign. Then he turned on his lights and headed home, his mind full of possibilities.

CHAPTER 12

Monday, June 24, 2003

It was 8:30 a.m., and Sean and Gerald were looking at videos taken at Sacred Heart Church the Saturday before. They were especially interested in any taken of the nuns who were in attendance entering the church, during the Mass, and exiting down the main aisle and the west exit of the church where the bathroom was located.

They first looked at the video of the camera that was located in the spray of flowers in front of the altar. They saw the nuns coming down the middle aisle toward the altar. They came in single file, genuflected, and entered a pew two rows behind where the readers would eventually sit. They were all dressed in black and white, although their habits were different. The third nun was taller than the other two and kept her head bowed most of the time. She looked up only when Kate read the first reading and Father Joe gave his homily. Neither Sean nor Gerald could tell by her face or facial expressions that she might have been a man. At times she lowered her head, squirmed a bit, and placed a handkerchief to her eyes as if emotion had taken over.

They watched as she left the pew and headed for the bathroom outside the side entrance, but this time they couldn't see her face.

Then they looked at the second video. It was from a camera located in the choir loft, which was positioned to view those walking down the main aisle away from the altar. Once again the nun kept her head down with a handkerchief over most of her face. She walked slowly, as if in no rush to leave the church.

As she walked through the door into the little room that held the door to the bathroom and another door to the outside, another camera picked up her movements. At this point she removed the handkerchief and a fairly good view of her face filled the screen. She entered into the bathroom. Five minutes later, a person emerged. It was no longer a nun. The heavy-set, bald man, dressed in a tan shirt and beige pants, looked into the camera apparently unaware that it was there. Under his arm was a rolled up article of black material, probably the nun's habit. To both Sean and Gerald it was quite evident by his facial expression that he was angry.

"Well, Gerald," Sean said. "I think we have a good look at the suspect. Does he look like anyone you've seen before in church?"

"No," Gerald said. "But perhaps Father Joe or Mrs. Shaw might recognize him."

They continued to look through the rest of the videos and were joined by the rest of the attending officers.

Seeing nothing else of importance, Sean told one of the officers to make hard copies of a number of shots of the nun/suspect to show Kate and Father Joe.

Sean decided to take home the first two videos to see if he could determine what caused their suspect to leave the church early. He told Gerald that he believed that Father Joe would be back on Wednesday, and he would set up a meeting with him as soon as he could. Sean would also invite Kate to view the photos.

Kate had gotten an early start with her walk and by eight o'clock was already on her way to the school. In the back seat of her car were three boxes, which she would fill with the contents of her desk and any remaining things of hers which were still in her classroom.

Jan would be coming in later in the morning, and they would stop for a snack and cup of coffee.

As Kate sat at her small desk for the last time, she reflected on how she came to be at Sacred Heart so many years ago. Andy had been having trouble in his second-grade classroom in the town where they lived. He had lost his initial enthusiasm for school and couldn't seem to concentrate on getting his work done.

A parishioner at Sacred Heart had told her about a small Catholic school in the next town, and Kate had decided a visit was in order. Delighted with what they had found, she and Ted made the commitment to send Andy there the following year. Although it meant driving him back and forth to school and paying tuition, they had never regretted the decision. Michael entered first grade at Sacred Heart the next year.

Kate helped out in the school, and when a teaching job opened up, the principal, Sister Mary Anne, hired her. Over the years she had taught a number of different grades, ending up as the third-grade teacher. She had never regretted that decision either.

How different it's going to be come September, thought Kate. *It won't hit me until August, when I would normally be getting ready for a new school year.*

Jan stuck her head through the doorway and interrupted her thoughts.

"How're ya doing, Kate?" Jan asked in her usual cheery voice. "I brought some coffee and goodies. Are you ready for a break?"

"Yes, I am," replied Kate. "I was sitting here just thinking about how I got here and how it will be come the fall."

"Well, you still plan on coming back as a volunteer, don't you, Kate?" asked Jan, handing her a cup of coffee. "It wouldn't be the same without you."

"Of course," said Kate, laughing. "There is only just so much cleaning one can do at home."

"I was wondering if you would be doing any camping this summer," Jan said as she pulled up a chair next to Kate.

"You know, Jan, even though the boys and I went up to the campgrounds and opened up the camper in May, I hadn't planned on going up until school got out. Ted and I had such good times up there, not only with the boys, but by ourselves, that I have a hard time thinking about being up there alone," said Kate wistfully.

"Maybe you should go up with someone the first time," suggested Jan.

"Would you and Scott like to go?" asked Kate.

"You know we'd love to," Jan answered. "Of course we could only go for a weekend because Scott can't get the time off during the week."

They continued discussing camping possibilities as Kate emptied out the last of her desk drawers. Then Jan helped her load the boxes into her car.

After Jan left, Kate looked around her room one last time to make sure everything of hers had been cleaned out. As she stood in the doorway, she once again thanked God for the years she had spent interacting with all the young people entrusted to her care. Because of her small salary, Ted had always teased her about her "hobby." But they both knew it was more a mission than a hobby. Others had asked her why she didn't go to teach in the public sector where the pay and benefits were substantially better, but she would always give the same answer: "I wouldn't be able to talk about Jesus each and every day and how important He is in our lives."

As she left the school, she was mentally going over the things she had to pick up at the grocery store for her lunch with Margot. So much so that she didn't notice the white car that followed her into the store parking lot. She got out of her car and walked into the store. The white car had parked a couple of rows away, and its occupant just sat there.

It took Kate about twenty minutes to make her selections and check out. As she exited the store, she noticed that the sky had started to cloud up. *I hope we're not going to get a shower,* she thought as she loaded her groceries into her car.

She needn't have worried, though, because by the time she reached her house the sky had cleared again.

While unloading her groceries, something caught her eye. She couldn't believe it! The flowers in the flower barrel on the left side of the garage were gone. Well not exactly, they were half-gone. To be precise, the tops were gone, leaving only the stems.

Kate stood there, her arms full of grocery bags, dumbfounded. *How could that have happened?*

Shaking her head, she brought her groceries inside and then went back out to inspect the flower barrel. The tops were gone! She decided that something, probably a deer, had had a wonderful lunch at her expense. Checking her other flower barrels, she found that they were fine.

She went back into the house to put away her groceries and prepare the lunch. She looked at the clock and saw that Margot would be there in an hour. *It will be so good to see and talk to her again,* she thought. Kate had just finished setting her table on her front porch when Margot pulled into her driveway.

Margot Green was a willowy ash-blonde with a whispery voice. Today she was dressed in a tan polo, white capris, and sandals. Although in her early fifties, she could pass for forty. She had been Kate's friend since college. Although an interior decorator, she had not worked since she had had children. Her husband, Paul, was an investment counselor in a prestigious firm. He made a good enough salary that they lived comfortably and were able to go on quite a few trips throughout the year.

"Kate, I hope you like this small gift I picked up for you in Rome," she said as she handed Kate the package.

"Oh, I'm sure I will," said Kate excitedly. "But more importantly, let me get a look at you," Kate said as she hugged Margot. "I'm so glad you're home." At that tears began to fall and the two friends continued to hug each other.

Together the two women brought out the lunch fixings, and over lunch Kate told Margot what she had been going through. Margot listened without interrupting, at times with a look of dismay. "I can see how this all has affected you, Kate. How terrible! I wish I had been here."

Kate replied that she was glad she wasn't and encouraged her to tell about her trip. The change of subject did them both good, and soon Kate opened her present. It was a beautiful, hand-carved music box.

The afternoon passed quickly as it does when close friends come together. As they ate dessert and drank their coffee, they got caught up on what was happening with their children and other family members.

Bob Stevens showed up mid-afternoon with the key to his mother's house and, after a few minutes, went on his way.

At four o'clock Margot's cell phone rang and after talking to her husband, she invited Kate to go out to dinner with them. As much as Kate wanted to go, she refused, saying she had to go to the nursing home to see Nellie and go to Nellie's house to feed her cat. Margot wouldn't take no for an answer, telling her that she would go with her. Then, after they had done what Kate needed to do, they would meet Paul at the restaurant. Kate, realizing that she really didn't want to be alone, gratefully accepted Margot's offer.

Before leaving she put in a call to Michael to tell him her plans and found out that Andy had gone over to their house for dinner. "Two birds with one stone," she told Michael.

As they walked to Margot's car, Margot noticed Kate's flower barrel. "What happened here, Kate? I didn't notice that when I came in!" exclaimed Margot.

"I think a deer had a late breakfast this morning," said Kate. They both had a good laugh over the thought of the deer eating the flowers. "I'll wait a few days and see if any grow back. If not, I'll replant them," Kate said.

Having fed Samantha, Kate and Margot headed for the nursing home.

They found Nellie sitting in her wheelchair next to her bed watching TV. She was so glad to see Kate, but although she had met Margot many times before, she had no memory of her. After they sat down, Nellie told them all about her move from the hospital and that her boys wouldn't be back until the weekend and then gave them information about her roommate, who, at that time, was not in the room. She was in a very good mood, and Kate got the impression that she was glad to be out of the hospital and in her new surroundings.

"I fed Samantha and changed her litter box before I came," Kate told Nellie. She also told her about the flower barrel incident.

"In all the years I've lived in my house, I never had that happen," said Nellie. Kate was surprised at this from Nellie, who had frequently complained about her flowers getting eaten the previous year, but she said nothing, chalking it up to Nellie's memory loss from the fall. Margot chimed in, regaling Nellie and Kate with stories of her experiences on her trip, and soon she had them in stitches. *Margot always was a good storyteller*, thought Kate.

Time passed, and soon they could hear the clanging of pans in the halls signaling dinnertime. An aide came in to help set up a table in front of Nellie for her dinner plates.

When delivered, the food looked hot and inviting, and Kate and Margot took their leave, with Kate telling Nellie that she'd see her the next day.

As Kate and Margot waited for the down elevator, Margot commented on how good Nellie looked despite her ordeal. They were busy talking to each other as they entered the elevator and didn't see who exited the one next to theirs.

He looked like any other visitor walking down the corridor. He stopped at room 102 and looked in. Seeing only Nellie, he entered slowly. "Excuse me, ma'am," he asked. "Is this Catherine Healy's room?"

Looking up from her supper, Nellie smiled and told him that it was not.

"Sorry to bother you, I'll have to ask at the nurses' station. Thank you," he said as he left. Once in the corridor again, he went to the elevator and pressed the down button. Only after he got on his elevator did he smile slightly. *She didn't recognize me*, he thought to himself. *That certainly simplifies things.*

At seven o' clock, Kate and Margot met Paul at a small restaurant known for its fine Italian cuisine. The three of them spent an evening full of reminiscing. At about ten, after coffee and dessert, Paul asked for the check, refusing any help with it from Kate. Looking at the two of them, she thanked God for such friends.

It was almost eleven when Kate finally said good-bye to Margot and Paul. As she unlocked the door to her kitchen, she could hear the phone ringing. It stopped just as she reached it. She returned to the doors and locked up again.

As she got ready for bed, she realized how tired she was and set her alarm for seven. *Guess I'll sleep in a bit,* she thought as her head hit the pillow.

Sean, too, was getting ready for bed. He had spent the last two hours watching the tapes of the memorial Mass. He had pretty much decided that the suspect had begun to get agitated during the first reading that Kate read and left his pew at the close of Father Joe's homily. The suspect, no matter how careful he was, couldn't help squirming or bringing his handkerchief to his face. Perhaps he was afraid either Kate or Father Joe might recognize him. Sean had decided that maybe they would. Wednesday couldn't come soon enough.

CHAPTER 13

Tuesday, June 25, 2003

Father Joe had risen early and already said his private Mass in his hotel room. Al's relatives had offered to put him up during his stay, but he had decided that they needed to grieve alone.

The funeral Mass had gone smoothly the previous day. Father Joe had con-celebrated with the pastor of the church where Al and his wife were married. Al was buried next to his wife in St. Anthony, a small town just outside Minneapolis, Minnesota. After the burial, all were invited back to the house of Al's nephew, Jeffrey, and his wife, Mary. There was a lot of reminiscing of happier times. No one brought up questions of Al's death, for which Father Joe was grateful. Many did say that Al had talked to them about how much he loved being at Sacred Heart. Father Joe got the impression that they thought of him as a dear friend of Al's. He was one of the first to leave but was invited back for supper the next day. When he returned to his hotel, he found he wasn't hungry, so he showered and settled in to watch some TV. Around nine, no longer able to keep his eyes open, he turned off the TV and said his prayers from his Breviary and went to bed.

Although tired, he did not sleep well. Reoccurring dreams of Kate and Al plagued him. Somehow they were connected. At one time, he awoke with a start and had trouble going back to sleep. Finally, he took out his rosary and prayed. He dozed off just before dawn.

After a continental breakfast courtesy of the hotel, Father Joe went for a walk, thinking it would clear his head. It was a clear day with no sign of rain. He sat on a bench in a nearby park and watched some children swinging and playing on seesaws and jungle gyms with their mothers close by. He envied their innocence and freedom from concern. He knew what was waiting him when he returned to Sacred Heart. At times, the burdens of being a pastor were heavy. Especially if one was the caretaker of a school in financial difficulty due to economic downturn and social changes.

As Father Joe continued to watch the children, he thought of Al. Al loved children but could never have any of his own. Pictures came to him of Al umpiring a game of kickball, being at one end of a turning rope, mediating an argument, even reprimanding some errant behavior. Always firm but fair. *How will I ever replace him, not just as a principal, but my friend?* He prayed for Al's soul.

Little by little, the playground emptied. That and a growling stomach told Father Joe that it was time for lunch. He walked around the neighborhood until he found a small café. Going in, he saw it had two- and four-person tables as well as a counter with stools. Choosing to sit at the counter, he was soon approached by a smiling young woman. "Hello, Father, what can I do for you today?" She handed him a menu and silverware wrapped in a paper napkin. He ordered a cup of decaf coffee and a grilled ham and cheese sandwich. Drinking his coffee, he noticed that there were very few people in the restaurant and wondered why. The prices were good and the café itself was clean. When his order came, he bowed his head and silently said grace.

As he was just finishing, the waitress came over and asked if he would like dessert and proceeded to tell him about the fresh apple pie that had been baked that morning. "I don't think I can pass that up!" said Father Joe, his spirits lifting. The pie proved to be as good as advertised.

Walking back to his hotel, Father Joe thanked God for sticking with him through his "down times." He decided that he would take a nap that afternoon so he would be fresh for supper.

Kate's day had started with her normal walk and "kitty duty." After she ate breakfast and washed the dishes, she stripped her bed and put in a load of wash. Today would be a good drying day.

Mid-morning, Kate made a cup of tea. She sat out on her deck with her tea, her newspaper, and a blueberry muffin. The sun was already warm, so she put up her table umbrella.

Wash done and hung out to dry, Kate made her bed and took her shower. She had decided she would go in to town and do some grocery shopping, and when she came back she would make some brownies to take with her to the nursing home.

Locking up her house and the mudroom doors, she went down the stairs to her car. Something was not right about her car! It didn't take her long to figure out that her passenger-side front tire was flat. She remembered that Ted always took care of things like that and tried to remember the last time she changed a tire. *It must have been when I was single*, she thought. When she checked the tire in the trunk, she found that it too was flat.

What do I do now? I guess I'll have to call AAA.

The AAA garage mechanic came, as promised, forty-five minutes later. Kate charged the cost of the new tire to her credit card. He made fast work of changing her flat and put it in her trunk. In no time at all, she was on her way to the grocery store. Along the way, she stopped at a tire place and dropped off both of the tires in her trunk to be inflated or repaired as the case might be.

As she was pushing her cart of groceries out of the store into the parking lot, she met a neighbor who was also a friend of Nellie. They talked for a few minutes about Nellie, and when they parted the neighbor told Kate that she would go and visit Nellie. Of course, Kate was happy to hear that. The more people who visited Nellie during the week the less lonely she would be.

Kate had carried the last of her groceries inside when the phone rang. "Mrs. Shaw, this is Mike at Nelson Tire," said the caller.

"Yes, Mike, I can't believe that you've fixed those tires so fast," said Kate.

"Well, no, I haven't exactly. That is what I'm calling you about," he answered. "One of the tires was no problem because it just needed some air, but I'm afraid the other one can't be repaired. It was punctured on the side somehow. There is no way to fix something like that." Stunned, Kate thanked him, told him she'd be up later to pick up the good tire, and hung up.

After she ate lunch and made a batch of brownies, Kate loaded the dishwasher with the dirty dishes and took chicken out of the freezer to have for supper. Brownies in hand, she locked up the house and headed out to the nursing home. On the way she stopped at the tire shop to pick up her good tire and to get more information about the tire that couldn't be repaired. In talking to Mike, she learned that the tire would have been unsafe, if not impossible, to drive upon. Troubled by that news, she paid her bill and continued on her way to see Nellie, all the way trying to think of where or how that tire got damaged.

Once again Nellie was in good spirits. She had been to physical and occupational therapy, had eaten lunch, and had taken a short nap. They had a good visit, reminiscing about when their sons were young. Nellie could recall those days but could not remember what she had eaten for lunch. Kate told her about her dinner the previous night with Margot and Paul. Finally, around four o'clock, Nellie started to nod off, and Kate told her she was leaving but would be back the next day.

As Kate was driving home she remembered the load of wash that was out on the line. *Good thing it stays light so late now.*

Once she had put a potato in the oven to bake and had changed, she got her clothesbasket and headed out to collect her clothes from the line. As she approached her clothesline, chills went through her body. Every piece of laundry on the line was lying flat on the ground. Kate dropped the basket where she stood and ran inside. Once there, she locked all the doors. She was shaking so badly that she had to sit down to calm herself. "My God," she asked aloud, "what in the world is happening?"

Kate thought of calling one of her boys when the phone rang. She hesitated before she picked up.

"Hello," she said cautiously.

"Hello, Mrs. Shaw, it's Sean Burke."

"Oh hello, Sergeant, I'm so glad it's you calling."

The tone of her voice made Sean sit straight up in his chair. "Is everything all right, Mrs. Shaw?"

"I'm really not sure, Sergeant," said Kate. "I suppose there is a logical explanation, but a number of unusual things have happened the last few days. Unsettling, really."

"Well, I was calling to see if you could attend a meeting with Father Joe tomorrow afternoon. I think we have pictures of a possible suspect. But now, maybe I should stop by so we can discuss what has gotten you so unnerved," said Sean.

Kate could hear the concern in his voice. "I really don't want to put you out over this when I'm not even sure it's anything," said Kate.

"It's no problem," said Sean. "Have you eaten yet? I haven't, and I was planning on picking up some Chinese. Would you like me to bring some for you too?"

"I can't tell you when I've had Chinese, and that sounds better than what I had in mind."

"Okay," said Sean, "I'll see you in about forty-five minutes."

After they had hung up, Sean called in his order, straightened out his desk, and headed out to his car. He sat for a minute wondering what had upset Kate so much. *Does she sense that she might in danger and doesn't want to tell her sons*?

Kate turned off her oven, put the chicken she was planning on having in the refrigerator, set her kitchen table, and got her coffee pot set up. She took out a cranberry loaf cake from the freezer and defrosted it in the microwave. She noticed that it was starting to get dark and turned her outside lights on. She decided not to unlock her doors until she was sure it was the sergeant who was at the door.

Kate sat in a living room chair and thought through all the things that had happened since Al's death that she had, up to now, brushed aside. She decided to make a list of those incidents in chronological order. She started the list with Al's death, the time, and the date. The first thing that happened after that was the problem with her newspaper tube. She didn't have the exact time of that, so she put a range of time in. She stopped and thought, *Should I put Nellie in here? Is she connected in some way?* Using a red pen, she made a question mark there. The thought of Nellie's attack somehow being an incident in a chain of events was almost too much to fathom. *Perhaps Sergeant Burke will give me some thoughts on this.*

Kate had just finished her list when the driveway beeper sounded. She felt a little better that at least she had something to show for her anxiety. She had also made the decision not to worry Michael or Andy.

Unlocking first her kitchen door and then her mudroom door, she kept Sean waiting a bit. He noticed right away that Kate wasn't herself.

Kate took the boxes of Chinese food from him and put them on the counter. "These smell delicious, Sergeant. What do you say we eat first and talk about our business later?" she asked Sean.

"That's fine with me," he responded. "What can I do to help?"

"Well, for starters tell me what you would like to drink and please take a seat," said Kate.

Sean had brought three entrées, and Kate put them in separate bowls. They both decided on iced tea. All three of the selections were still warm and tasty. They made small talk over their meal. Slowly, the uneasiness that Kate had felt earlier melted away. Somehow, she felt safe with Sean. She realized that that was one of the things she missed. Sean helped her clear the table and then, as asked, took a seat in her living room while she made the coffee. He had chosen the sofa and had spread the photos that his fellow officers had developed for him out on the coffee table in the order in which they were taken. He kept the final one in the original envelope.

When Kate had taken her seat on the sofa, he explained how the pictures had been taken. Kate was astounded that the pictures were of a nun until she looked at the one of the suspect in the small entryway where the bathroom was. When Sean finally showed her the last picture, she was sure that she had seen the man before. She couldn't get over the cleverness of the disguise. "But Sergeant, why would he go to all that trouble to be there?" she asked.

"Often times, a killer will return to the scene of his crime, to a church service, or even to a cemetery burial. The reasons may be different," said Sean quietly, "depending on the motive for the murder."

After they sat for a few minutes, Sean asked, "Do you think you could put a name with that face, Mrs. Shaw?"

"You know, Sergeant, he looks familiar, but I just can't come up with a name. Maybe if I pray on it, it will come to me."

"Well," Sean said. "That may happen tomorrow when we meet with Father Joe. Now, what was it that was bothering you, Mrs. Shaw?"

He watched as she reached into her pocket and took out a folded piece of paper. She opened it slowly and explained what she had done. "All of these could be explained away, Sergeant, until today. Things like these happen over time and mean nothing, but this afternoon when I went out to take in my wash…well, that couldn't be explained away. Someone had intentionally taken every piece of laundry off my clothesline and laid them flat on the grass." As Kate said this, Sean could see not only the tears but also the fear in her eyes. "I didn't list the hang-up calls I've been getting at all hours," she added.

Sean took his time reading through what he recognized as a well-thought-out, documented list.

"What is the red question mark for?" he asked.

"I didn't know if I should put Nellie in there," said Kate quietly. He sat for a moment, trying to decide how much he should tell her.

"I think, Mrs. Shaw, that you have every reason to be worried."

He went on to tell her his suspicions about Ted's accident, Al's murder, and Nellie's attack being somehow connected.

At first, she said nothing, refusing to believe that Ted's accident could have anything to do with recent happenings. Sean waited. He could almost hear wheels turning, rubber burning.

"Oh my God," she said finally. "The beeper!"

She explained that something had eluded her on the day of Ted's death. She had come down her driveway and had driven into her garage as per usual. She had seen Ted carrying an armload of wood down into the cellar hatchway as she had driven down the driveway. She had taken her book bag and a box that she had brought home from school into the mudroom. Leaving the box in the mudroom, she had gone into the house. She had gone past the cellar stairway, hollering down that she was home. From there, she had gone into the bathroom, dropping her book bag at the door. Then she had headed toward the bedroom to change. On the way, the phone had rung, and she had answered it in the den. At the time she had thought it was a wrong number because whoever it was had hung up. She had changed and once again had hollered down to Ted. No answer.

She had started for the mudroom door, and as she had opened it, she had heard the driveway beeper. She had gone into the mudroom and had retrieved the box that she had brought home from school and had brought it into the house. Then she had gone out to see Ted.

As she had walked out of the garage, she had looked down the driveway and had seen just the red taillight of a car that had turned right out of her driveway. Not thinking much about it, she had gone to look for Ted and had made that horrible discovery.

At this point, tears streamed down her face, and Sean reached into his back pocket and handed her his handkerchief. He wanted to hold her and tell her it would be all right, but he knew it wasn't his place.

"It wasn't an accident, was it?" she finally asked.

Sean answered, "Upon closer inspection of the autopsy report, we think he was hit from behind with some kind of club. That, and the fall with his head striking the metal edge of the top step killed him. He probably died almost instantly. Because it appeared to be an accident, the investigation didn't go any further. What do you say we take a break and have some of that delicious-smelling coffee, Mrs. Shaw?"

With that, they stood up and went into the kitchen. Kate got the cups, saucers, and dessert plates. Sean sat at his place at the table. She brought over the silverware and poured the coffee, taking her place opposite him. She handed him his handkerchief. "I'm so sorry. I guess I got it all wet," she said.

"That's understandable," he replied. "I'm just glad I had one to give you."

At that, Kate smiled. Then she got up and got the milk pitcher, the sugar bowl, and the dessert. They ate their dessert and drank their coffee for a few minutes without talking. "So, you think that this might be the man who killed Al and my Ted, Sergeant?" Kate asked quietly.

"It's a good possibility," Sean replied. "It's also possible that he was responsible for Nellie's fall and for the attempts that have been made to frighten you."

Sean could see her face change. A look of resignation flickered across it. "I guess I will be next?" she asked.

"We don't know for sure, Mrs. Shaw," answered Sean. "I can assure you, we'll do all we can to protect you."

"What about my children?"

"I've already arranged to have them watched, without their knowledge, of course."

"Thank you so much, Sergeant," Kate said, on the verge of tearing up again. But she held back.

Sean continued to tell her about the direction of the investigation. "Once we get a name to go with that face, and we're hoping Father Joe will be able to supply one, we'll put out an APB on him and bring him in," he said.

"What should I do?" asked Kate.

"Well," said Sean, "I'd like you to keep your cell phone on your person at all times. You do have one, don't you?"

"I have Ted's," said Kate. "I'm not sure how it works, though."

"I'll look at it in a moment," said Sean. "Secondly, keep your doors and windows locked at all times. Third, be aware of everything around you, and if you think anyone is following you or you're uneasy about anything, call. Now let me look at that phone."

After charging the cell phone, Sean gave her a quick lesson on how to use it. He programmed in his cell phone number and had her call him. At her request, he programmed in both her sons' numbers.

"Now, Mrs. Shaw, I want you to call me every day, three times a day, the last being before you go to bed at night," he said. "I want you to get used to using it."

"Sergeant, I feel as if this is an awful imposition," Kate said.

Sean looked straight into her blue eyes and said, "Mrs. Shaw, it's no imposition at all. After all, it's my job to protect you and to catch this killer."

"I see," Kate said thoughtfully. "But if we're going to be talking this often, how about calling me Kate?"

Sean didn't hesitate when he said, "Only if you call me Sean."

"It's a deal, Sean," she said.

They cleared off the table, and Kate agreed, at Sean's coaxing, to tell her sons what was going on. He also told her that there would be a cruiser posted at the end of the driveway as soon as he put a call in, which he did when she excused herself to go to the bathroom. Then he scooped up his photos and put them in his pocket.

It was nine-thirty when Sean left. Sean waved at the officer who pulled up next to Kate's driveway just as he reached the end of it. He got out of his car, went over, explained the situation, and gave the officer Kate's cell phone number.

Kate called Michael first, knowing that he and Elizabeth liked to be in bed by ten. She invited them for supper the following night, telling Michael she had some news to share.

"That's great, Mom, we have some news to share too," he said.

Then she called Andy and said the same.

Sean drove home thinking about how brave Kate had been when hearing the news. Nellie came to mind, and Sean could have kicked himself for forgetting to tell Kate that Nellie, too, had police protection. *Oh, well, I'll tell her tomorrow when we meet with Father Joe*, he thought to himself.

When he got home, he found the light blinking on his answering machine. It was Father Joe telling him he would be on an early flight and would telephone him as soon as he touched down at the airport.

Kate's exhaustion was based on the emotions she felt. On the one hand, the blame she had shouldered concerning Ted's death, namely that there must have been something she could have done to prevent it, had lifted. On the other hand, the overwhelming confusion and sorrow over why it happened hit her heavily. She realized that the burden of telling her children that their father had been murdered, and not being able to tell why, was hers alone. Maybe she should have asked Sean to come to dinner, too and let him tell them in case they had questions. *No,* she told herself, *it's my job*.

Just as she was getting into bed, her cell phone rang. "Hello, Mrs. Shaw, this is Officer Dale Young. I was just checking in to see if all was okay. I'm parked on the street next to your driveway."

"Thank you so much, Officer," said Kate, "it seems fine here."

"Okay, Mrs. Shaw, try to get some sleep now," he said.

After they had hung up Kate put the phone next to her bed. She knew she wouldn't get much sleep.

While Officer Young was talking to Kate, a white car passed by.

She finally caught on to my "messages," he thought. *Well, that patrol car won't stop me. In fact, it might help.*

It wasn't long before he was at the other neighborhood. Once again the blue car entered the driveway, and a woman entered the house. Shortly afterward, a teenager left the house and walked home. *Your time is short,* he said to himself as the lights in the small ranch went out.

CHAPTER 14

Wednesday, June 26, 2003

After a nightmare-filled night and many wake-ups, Kate finally got out of bed. She decided to forego her walk, grabbed her clothes and her cell phone, and went in to take her shower. As the hot water cascaded over her body, she felt the tenseness ease. She stayed in longer than she usually did. When she finally toweled off, she noticed her skin was pink. After dressing in sweats, she slipped her phone into her pants pocket.

The sun was just coming up, and there was a mist close to the ground when she walked up her driveway. She could see the cruiser sitting at the end of the driveway. Officer Young got out of his cruiser when he saw Kate coming. "Good Morning, Mrs. Shaw," he said cheerily. "You're up early."

"I tried to sleep but couldn't. I'm on my way to feed my neighbor's cat."

"Well, my orders are to stick like glue to you, and my legs could use some exercise. So I guess that means I get to meet your neighbor's cat," he said with a smile. Kate knew better than to argue. The two of them walked up to Nellie's house, exchanging small talk along the way.

Samantha was at the door waiting for Kate, but when she saw Officer Young she scurried into the other room. Kate assured him that she was that way with anyone she didn't know and proceeded to change her water and fill her dish with fresh cat food. Then she changed the kitty litter box.

The officer walked around the house, looking at pictures on the walls and knickknacks on various shelves. Everything was neat and only slightly dusty.

Soon they were walking back to Kate's driveway. "How about some breakfast, Officer?" Kate asked.

"That sounds so good, Mrs. Shaw, but I really don't want to impose," Officer Young answered.

"You know it would be great to have company for breakfast," said Kate. "Usually I'm stuck eating alone."

"Well, if you put it that way, I could go for a cup of coffee." Kate told him she would walk down, and he could follow her in his cruiser rather than leave it in the road. She waited at her mudroom door for him while he called in on his car phone and told whoever was in charge where he would be. She unlocked that door and the one to her kitchen.

Once inside, Kate persuaded him to have some scrambled eggs and toast with his coffee. They talked about their families. Dale Young was the proud father of two young boys and regaled Kate with amusing stories about them. She told Dale that she was waiting until eight to check in with Sean. Dale told her that another officer would be here to take his place shortly.

They were just finishing up when they heard the driveway beeper go off, telling them that someone was coming down the driveway. Dale told Kate that he would check to see if it was his replacement and as he left, told her to lock the door behind him.

Sure enough, it was Officer Ronald Greer. The two officers went back into the house, where Dale introduced his replacement. Ronald was talked into having a fresh cup of coffee before he went out to take his post. Kate told him that she would be going into town for a meeting at the church office with Father Joe and Sergeant Burke, but she didn't know at what time. Officer Greer asked for her cell phone and programmed in his number.

Before both men left, they thanked her for her hospitality. Dale was on his way home, and Ronald drove to the end of the driveway and parked on the street. The beeper sounded the alarm as both cruisers passed. Kate locked her doors.

Kate cleaned the kitchen and poured herself a second cup of coffee. She thought to herself that she would never hear that beeper again without thinking of Ted. After she had checked in with Sean, she went out to collect her wash that was still on the ground. Having rewashed it, she dried it in the dryer this time.

Father Joe had made it to the airport in plenty of time for his 8:00 a.m. flight. He was glad that he had been able to get a direct flight home, because he wanted to get back as soon as he could. He decided that he would call Sergeant Burke as soon as he was in his car and set up a time for their meeting. He was hoping the sergeant had some insights into Al's murder. *Could the cameras that had been placed strategically in the church have photographed a suspect? Would it be someone I would recognize?* He leaned back in his seat and fingered the rosary beads that were in his pocket. *At least it's quiet on this flight.*

The flight was uneventful and on time. Father Joe could go straight to the shuttle that would bring him to where his car was parked. He paid the attendant and walked to his car.

The bright sunshine lifted his spirits, and he decided to stop along the way home and buy a cup of coffee and a donut. Sitting in the car with his purchase, he didn't notice that a blue car had followed him from the parking area at the airport and had parked on the other side of this parking lot.

After Father Joe had eaten his donut, he called Sergeant Burke, who was pleased to hear from him. They decided on a two-thirty meeting at the church office and that Sean would call Kate to let her know. Sean told Father Joe how he had decided to protect Kate after hearing about various incidents. Father Joe was surprised about what she had been going through, as she hadn't mentioned anything.

"I don't think she realized they were anything important until the laundry thing," said Sean.

"Kate, being who she is, would find it difficult to imagine that anyone could be so evil," said Father Joe. "I'm glad you're looking out for her safety, Sergeant."

The ride home consisted of one-lane traffic in both directions along very curvy up-and-down hills. In places there weren't any guardrails, even though there were steep drop-offs. The speed limit was only thirty to forty in most places, and passing was prohibited. Fortunately, there was very little traffic at that time of day. Father Joe's thoughts were on the earlier conversation with Sean. Suddenly, he looked in his rearview mirror and saw a blue car closing in on him. When they drove along a stretch of road that had sharp curves, the car behind Father Joe closed the gap and was almost on his bumper.

Father Joe started to look for a place to pull over, the thought going through his mind that the person behind him must be in an awful hurry. Then he noticed a car coming in the opposite direction. The car in back of him seemed to slow down, and Father Joe let out a sigh of relief. But it wasn't long before the blue car was tailgating again. Then he dropped back again.

As they reached an especially steep downhill part of the road, the blue car rammed the back of Father Joe's car. The crunching sound of metal meeting metal was deafening. Father Joe had all he could do to keep control of the car. He went as close to the edge of the road as he dared, hoping the other car would pass him.

Pass him it did. But as it did, the driver sideswiped the side of Father Joe's car, shattering the window next to him and sending it off the side of the road. Tumbling over and over, down the side of the hill, Father Joe's head slammed against the steering wheel. Just before he lost consciousness, he heard glass breaking and metal snapping around him and smelled smoke. The car finally came to rest on the passenger side.

The driver of the blue car could not see Father Joe's car any longer and didn't take the time to stop. About four miles down the road he entered a small boat-landing parking area that bordered on a quiet lake. Parking his car, he got out and walked to a white car parked nearby, got in, and drove away satisfied with his day's work.

What he hadn't seen in his rush to get away undetected was the woman in a grey car who had come around a curve just as his car had pushed Father Joe's car over the edge of the road. She had stopped her car and immediately called 911. She could see smoke rising from below. She grabbed a first-aid kit out of her glove compartment, jumped out of her car, took a blanket off of her back seat, and made her way down the hill through glass and pieces of metal that had belonged to Father Joe's car.

Sally Warner, a nurse, had been coming home after her shift in the nearby clinic when she saw the "accident." When she reached the car, she saw that it was lying on the passenger side with smoke coming from under the hood. She could hear sirens in the distance. The driver's side of the car was badly crumpled with all the windows smashed, but she tried to get the driver's side door open anyway. At first it wouldn't budge but then opened enough for her to get to the victim. She saw that the occupant, a priest, had a head injury, and she checked for a pulse. Although unconscious, he was breathing regularly and his pulse was just a bit elevated. With her first-aid kit, she bandaged his head wound and put the blanket around him as much as possible to keep him warm in case of internal injuries, talking to him all the while. Then she headed back up the hill to meet the paramedics.

Sean was at his desk when news of Father Joe's accident came in. He yelled for Gerald, and the two of them went to the scene. They arrived just as Father Joe was being loaded into an ambulance. Sean hardly recognized him. Father Joe had on a neck brace, and his head was wrapped in bandages. His face was black and blue and covered with abrasions. Without thinking, Sean said a prayer for him.

Nearby, a woman wearing a nurse's uniform stood next to her car, holding a cup of coffee. Gerald went down the hill to examine the crash site, while Sean approached Sally Warner. After introductions, he thanked her for stopping to help and then asked if he could take a statement from her. As the ambulance left, they went to sit in Sean's cruiser. Sally told Sean what she had seen happen. "I just couldn't believe what I was seeing, Sergeant," she said. "This blue car looked like it was passing the priest and then rammed the side of his car. I think it was on purpose."

"Did you get a look at the license plate, Ms. Warner?" Sean asked.

"No, I'm sorry, I just wanted to call for help and get to the crash site as soon as I could. I was sure whoever was in that car didn't make it. I'm so glad I was wrong," she answered. "I think the car might have been a Dodge, though, because it looked somewhat like my brother's car."

Finished with his questioning, Sean gave Sally his card and, thanking her again, asked her to call him if she thought of anything else. Then he went down to the crash scene to join Gerald and the other officers who were there.

"I don't know how Father Joe survived this crash, Sergeant," said Gerald, shaking his head.

"We don't know that he has yet, Gerald," said Sean. "He definitely didn't look all that well."

They looked at the badly damaged car and then climbed up to the road, leaving the other officers to finish up.

Once in the cruiser, Sean gave Gerald Sally Warner's statement to read. They decided that he and Gerald would go to the church office to tell the secretary, Margaret McClellan, about Father Joe's accident rather than calling her.

In the church office, Margaret immediately could tell by their faces that this was not a courtesy call.

"Mrs. McClellan, I'm sorry to have to tell you, but Father Joe has been in an auto accident and has been transported to Memorial Hospital," said Sean.

"Oh my God," said Margaret, with a stricken look on her face.

"We don't know his condition yet, Mrs. McClellan."

"I'll call the answering service and close the office. Then I'll head right up there," said Margaret.

As Sean opened the door to his cruiser, he remembered Kate. He was sure she would want to go to the hospital. He told Gerald that he would drop him off at the station, go get Kate, and bring her to the hospital.

Kate was watering one of her flower barrels when she looked down her driveway and saw not one but two cruisers at the end of her driveway. Then one came down her driveway and the other left. She was surprised to see Sean getting out of the cruiser. Right away, she thought about her sons. She walked toward the cruiser. She could see by his face that it wasn't good news.

Almost as if Sean could read her mind, he prefaced his news with, "Don't worry, Kate, your boys are okay, but I do have some bad news for you. Father Joe was in an accident on the way home from the airport. He's been taken to Memorial Hospital."

"Is it serious?" asked Kate.

"I'm not sure, but I thought you might like to go with me to the hospital," answered Sean. "I'll tell you what I know on the way."

On the way to the hospital, Sean told her what he knew about the accident.

Soon Sean and Kate entered the ER, and Sean went to the desk, while Kate went into the waiting room. There she found Margaret. In answer to her inquiries, Margaret told Kate that she had no news. By the time Margaret arrived, Father Joe had been checked over and was taken to be X-rayed.

Sean came back with more news. Father Joe had been moved to the ICU for observation. They could go up to the ICU floor but could only go in one at a time. This news hit Kate hard. She had been on vigil outside an ICU just over a week ago.

When Sean, Kate, and Margaret got off the elevator, they were met by a doctor who introduced himself as Dr. Griffin. He told them that Father Joe was conscious, and other than a bad gash to his head and possible concussion, he had no other injuries. They wanted to keep him in the ICU overnight to keep a close eye on him. Dr. Griffin also told them they could go in one at a time, even though only family was usually allowed.

After each had a chance to see Father Joe, they left together. Margaret got in her car and headed home. Kate and Sean got in his cruiser and headed toward Kate's house.

"Sean, if this person is going after Father Joe and me, isn't it possible that Nellie is in danger?" Kate asked.

"We do have an undercover officer in the nursing home, Kate, just in case," Sean answered. "I don't know why Nellie is involved, but no sense taking any chances."

"I was thinking about that, Sean. I know that the day Al was killed, someone pulled my newspaper tube out of the ground. I wonder if the killer might have done it in a rage. Maybe Nellie was driving by and saw him, and he tried to keep her quiet. He could have pushed her down the stairs in the hopes that it would kill her and still look like an accident."

"It's a possibility," said Sean.

When Sean turned into her driveway, Kate noticed that Dale Young's cruiser was parked in front of her garage. As they pulled up, he came walking around the side of her house. He came to Sean's cruiser to talk to the two of them. Sean updated him on news about Father Joe.

"He's getting more reckless, Dale, so you will really need to keep a look out," said Sean. Dale just nodded and got back into his cruiser and drove up the driveway to where he was parked the previous night.

Sean was getting ready to go. Kate invited him for supper, telling him that she had invited her sons and that she was hoping that he would be willing to talk to them with her about the danger facing her. He was glad for the invitation and told her he would be back around six.

Once inside, Kate called the nursing home to have them tell Nellie that she would not be in to visit her until tomorrow. After all that had happened, she just wasn't up to it. After eating some lunch, Kate felt better. She sat in her recliner to say a rosary for Father Joe. She *dozed* off, and an hour passed by before she woke with a start. She couldn't remember the last time she took a nap during the day.

Andy was the first to arrive at 5:30, followed shortly by Michael and Elizabeth. They all were surprised by the cruiser sitting at the end of the driveway. Kate told them that Sergeant Burke was coming for supper, and he would answer all their questions. Elizabeth put the dessert she had brought in the fridge.

They all went out on the front porch and sat at the table there, except Andy, who was getting everyone drinks. When Andy joined them, Kate told them about Father Joe. Michael, especially, was shocked. "Why are these things happening to Sacred Heart people?" asked Michael.

Kate told them that that was why Sergeant Burke was coming to supper—to explain his theories. The subject changed to lighter topics, namely, the golfing efforts of both Andy and Michael.

About the time they had finished their drinks, they heard a car pulling into the yard. Andy and Michael went to meet Sergeant Burke as he got out of his car. Kate and Elizabeth went inside to check on the supper.

After Kate's sons reintroduced themselves to Sean, the three men went inside. Michael introduced Elizabeth to Sean and asked him if he could get him a drink of iced tea or soda.

"Either one would be great, Michael," said Sean.

Kate was busy putting the roast on a platter and scooping the vegetables into a bowl. Then she cut the roast up into serving pieces and placed the platter on the table. Elizabeth followed with the vegetables. "I hope you all have good appetites tonight," Kate said. Sean remarked that everything smelled delicious. Everyone agreed. The last things to be put on the table were the salad and an assortment of salad dressings.

They all sat down, and Andy said grace: "Thank you, Lord, for family and friends and this wonderful meal."

They all chimed in with "Amen."

Sean couldn't get over how delicious the meal was and told the group that Kate's cooking sure beat his cooking or fast food. "I'm just glad that I have plenty of mouths to feed," Kate said. "It's really hard to cook a meal like this for one." As they ate, Sean engaged Kate's family in light conversation surrounding jobs and interests. Kate was so pleased at how well they got along.

Afterward, since it was still light out, Michael, Andy, and Sean went to sit on the porch while Elizabeth and Kate cleared off the table and readied it for the dessert course. When the coffee was done and Elizabeth had dished out her dessert, Kate called the men back in. Over dessert and coffee, Sean explained his theories and what the police were doing about them. Needless to say, Kate's family was taken aback by the fact that Sean believed that Ted had been murdered and that their mother's safety was in question. Sean assured them that everything was being done to protect them all.

Finally, Michael spoke, "Maybe you should come to live with us until this is all over, Mom."

"Thank you, Son, but I wouldn't want to upset your routine or put you and Elizabeth in any danger. Besides, I really need to be here for Nellie. I feed her cat and take in her mail every day and, of course, visit her."

Rather than argue with her, Michael turned to Sean. "What do you think, Sergeant?" he asked.

"I think your mother has to do what she feels comfortable with, Michael," answered Sean. "As I told you, you are all under surveillance." He also added that as soon as Father Joe felt up to it, he planned on showing him the photos of the suspect. In the meantime, officers would again question neighbors around the church to see if any saw the suspect leave the church or get in a car.

By the time they had finished dessert, coffee, and conversation, it was after nine. Michael and Elizabeth were the first to leave, with Sean and Andy following soon after. Kate made sure to lock herself in.

Kate cleaned up the dessert dishes. Her dishwasher was full. She tried to remember the last time that had happened. *Once this is over I'm definitely going to have friends over more often for dinner*. She turned the dishwasher on and went to brush her teeth and change into her pajamas. Then she remembered that Michael had said that he and Elizabeth had something to tell her. She'd have to remember to ask them what it was when she talked to them again.

She wondered if she would get a better night's sleep than the night before because she knew she was probably more tired. She climbed into bed and gave Sean a quick call to let him know she was settling in. He was glad to hear from her and thanked her again for supper. She put her cell phone on the night table next to her bed and turned out the lights. Amazingly, she was asleep soon after her head hit the pillow.

He stayed up for the news. There was nothing on about the priest. *Could it be that no one found his car*? He wondered. Slowly he began to work himself into a rage. *The priest deserved what he got. He shouldn't have been so friendly with the incompetent principal and teacher.* He turned off the TV and the lights and sat there in the dark, a gun clenched in his hand.

CHAPTER 15

Thursday, June 27, 2003

Margaret was hard at work on the church bulletin when the call came in from the hospital. She had come in much earlier than usual because there was no way she would get any sleep. She wanted to get the bulletin finished because she was hoping to be able to pick up Father Joe.

Father Joe's housekeeper, Irma Hudson, had been alerted about his accident and was in early too, hoping he would be released that day. Irma had changed his bedclothes and had put in a wash. She was busy putting together the ingredients of Father Joe's favorite dessert when the intercom to the church office beeped.

"Irma," said Margaret. "The hospital just called. Father Joe has been moved to a regular room, but they want to keep him one more night."

"I'm glad you called, Margaret," said Irma. "I'm just ready to bake his lemon squares. I guess we'll have to bring them with us to the hospital when we visit. Do you know when you'll be able to go?"

When they had spoken the day before, Margaret and Irma had decided to go to visit Father Joe together if he wasn't able to come home. "I think I'll be done with things around here shortly after noon, Irma. I'll catch a quick bite and then we can go." That was fine with Irma, who did not like to drive in the city and was glad that Margaret had offered to drive. They both hung up and went about their jobs.

By 7:30 a.m. Patricia Lawler had all four of her children's lunches packed. The kids were in their rooms putting the things that they couldn't do without into their backpacks. Excitement reigned. Today was the first day of summer day camp.

As they filed in to the kitchen for breakfast, Patricia asked if they had the necessities: suntan lotion, bug spray, rain jackets, and anything else she could think of. Camp was old hat to the older three, but it was the first year for the youngest child, Emily.

After breakfast, Patricia gave them their lunches and juice drinks, which they put in their backpacks as well. Then they all headed out to the car.

As they drove to the camp, Patricia noticed that a black car had pulled in back of them. She would not have been concerned, because the car didn't look familiar to her. Twenty minutes later she turned into the driveway of Shady Park Campground, where the summer camp was being held. The black car, which had been behind her, had continued on.

Once her kids registered, Patricia left for work. She didn't notice the black car returning and turning into the park. Instead, she felt glad that she finally could provide her "gang" with a little summer fun. She continued on her way to her job. With the uncertain economic times, one thing she couldn't do was miss work. Being a single parent of four, she always had some unexpected expense that would come up. She couldn't expect, and didn't want, any financial help from her children's father. She was just as glad that he was out of their lives.

He parked his car so that he could see children coming and going from the large building that served as a lunchroom.

He was glad he had followed Patricia here previously and decided to inquire about the camp for his "son" after she had left. He had worn a baseball cap and used his most congenial personality. Telling the camp counselor that he was a widower and was concerned about how his young son would adjust to a full day of camp, he was able to gain sympathy. The camp counselor went out of her way to show him around to all the areas in the park that would be used by the campers and gave him a booklet that gave even more information about scheduling and activities. He had assured her that he would return the following week with his son in tow.

Of course, he had no intention of really sending a son to summer camp. He was only interested in one summer camper: Emily Lawler. As he sat in his car, he saw a group of children filing into the lunchroom building and was pleased to see that Emily was among them. She had grown a little taller, and her hair was a little longer than when he had last seen her.

With that, he started his car as if ready to pull out. Last thing he needed was for anyone to become suspicious of his presence. As he drove out, his anger grew. *Why should I be deprived of my daughter? I love her dearly and need her.* Then his thoughts went to Kate. *So she has a police guard does she?* He knew he would have no trouble gaining entry to her house with or without the guard. After all, he had studied her habits carefully. He had been to her house a number of times and knew how to gain entry undetected.

Retired policeman Walter Brown had pulled into the boat landing at dawn and was surprised to see a blue car already parked there.

He backed his boat into the loading space next to the landing and got out of his car. As he glanced over at the other car, he noticed that it had significant damage on the passenger side, as if it had sideswiped another car. He unhooked his boat from the trailer and slid it farther into the water, tying it to a post. Then he parked his car and walked back to his boat. He climbed in, untied the rope holding the boat to the pier, and shoved off for a morning of fishing.

Three hours later, Walter returned to the pier and found the blue car still there. He was thrilled with his catch for the day, and his mouth was already watering in anticipation of supper. His wife, Dorothy, was a wonderful cook who had many fish recipes. After he had loaded his boat onto his trailer, he put in a call to his wife to tell her about the fish. No answer. *Probably out shopping*, he thought to himself.

Something about that beat-up car bothered him. He decided to call his friend Sean at the police station to tell him about it. First, though, he wanted to tell Sean about his fishing experience and invite him over for supper.

In no time Sean had the name of the owner of the car and had dispatched a cruiser to the man's house. Unfortunately, they reported back that the man was an elderly widower in a wheelchair. Evidently, his car, which he no longer drove, had been taken from his garage without his knowledge. *Another dead end*, thought Sean.

Kate had slept much better and woke somewhat refreshed. After her shower she dressed, put on coffee, and once again went up the driveway toward Dale's cruiser. Once again they walked together to Nellie's house, and Kate took care of her kitty duties. Then as they walked down to her house, Kate told Dale about her plans for the day. She would be out most of the day. She planned on going to see Nellie in the morning and Father Joe in the afternoon. She was also going to try to catch up with Jan for lunch.

As they entered the kitchen, Dale walked through the house ahead of Kate to check out all the rooms and the basement. All was in order. He refused her offer of breakfast but did sit down for a cup of coffee. The driveway beeper beeped, and soon they were joined by Ronald, Dale's replacement. When Ronald heard of Kate's plans, he was glad because he wanted to get back to the station to catch up on some paperwork. Dale, who looked tired, was glad to go home and get some rest. Ronald told Kate that he would be back on duty by four. The two young officers left together.

Kate called the hospital and found out that Father Joe was not going to be released until the next day but that he was out of intensive care. Then she cleaned up her kitchen and did the dishes, leaving them to dry in the dish drain.

At nine she called Jan, who was glad to go to lunch with her. They would meet at their favorite café "Soup and Nuts."

As soon as she had hung up, Michael called, checking to see how she was and once again asking her to come stay with him and Elizabeth. Kate told him how well things had been going and not to worry. She felt the police had things under control. She also told him her plans for the day and that she was going to call Andy when they were done talking, which she did.

By nine-thirty Kate was out the door and on her way to the nursing home. She found Nellie in good spirits, sitting up in her wheelchair. She told Nellie about her lunch date with Jan and that she had to visit a friend in the hospital that afternoon. She had decided before she had arrived that Nellie didn't need to know about Father Joe's close call. They had a nice visit until noon, when Nellie's lunch came. Kate told her that she would return the next day and left to meet Jan.

Over lunch, Kate told Jan what she knew about Father Joe's accident and swore her to secrecy. Better that the perpetrator not know that Father Joe had been found alive.

After lunch with Jan, Kate went to the hospital and, to her surprise, found a feisty Father Joe sitting up in bed, complaining about being held prisoner. Margaret was patiently explaining to him that his staying another day was a precaution and that she would be back first thing in the morning to pick him up.

"I guess you're not in the mood for this hot fudge sundae that I picked up for you, Father," said Kate, smiling.

"As if they'd let me have it, Kate," he said sadly.

"Oh, but they will, Father," Kate answered as she handed him the sundae and a napkin and spoon. "I checked at the desk before I came."

Margaret smiled and told the priest that now that the reinforcements were here, she and Irma would go along. She would see him in the morning. He waved his spoon at them, and they left.

Kate took a seat nearby, anxious to hear about his stay and tell him any news that she thought he wouldn't have heard.

Behind her, though, she heard a hearty, unmistakable voice. "Eating ice cream, Father?" Sean asked as he came through the door. "And giving everyone a hard time?"

"Who, me? Would I do that, Sergeant?" answered Father Joe, chuckling.

"I'm glad to find you in such good shape, Father," said Sean in a much more serious tone. "When are you going home?"

Father Joe told him the sooner the better.

Sean told Father Joe that they definitely found a suspect by using the cameras in church and that most likely it was the same man who forced his car off the road. Sean wanted to question him about the accident but thought that could wait.

Father Joe just nodded his head, marveled once again that he was still with them, and thanked God. When Father Joe looked like he was tiring, Sean and Kate said they needed to be getting along and left together. Father Joe nodded off before they reached the elevator.

"I think the accident took more out of him than he will admit," said Kate. Sean agreed.

Sean thought of asking Kate out for a cup of coffee but decided against it. They went their separate ways—Kate to her house and Sean to his friend Walter's house for supper.

It was after four o'clock when Kate approached her driveway. Ronald was at his post and waved at her as she pulled in.

Once inside, she locked herself in and went to get changed into something more comfortable.

While Kate was eating her supper, she thought she heard a noise in her basement, so she got up and locked the door to the basement. *This whole thing has got me so jittery that I'm letting my imagination run away with me. But on second thought, it might not be a bad idea to call down to Officer Greer and have him come up and take a look around.*

Kate took her cell phone out of her pocket and called Ronald. She told him about the noises she heard in her basement, and he said he'd be right down. In a few minutes, Kate heard the beep on the driveway, and when she saw him approaching the mudroom door, she went out to unlock it for him.

"I'm sorry, Officer," said Kate, as he came in. "It's probably just my imagination."

"Don't apologize, Mrs. Shaw," he replied. "That's just what you're supposed to do."

As he started down the steps to the basement, he told her to lock the basement door behind him and that he would call to her to let him back in. She did as she was told and went back to finish her supper, but found that she couldn't eat. She put water on for tea and cleared off the table.

After the basement door was closed, Ronald took his gun out of his holster and unhooked a flashlight from his belt. He slowly went down the stairs, shining the flashlight in front of him. He had turned on the lights, but there were some dark corners where someone could hide, and he wanted no surprises. He slowly searched the basement, looking under Ted's workbench and in wood boxes and examining the basement windows. He noticed that the keys to the outdoor hatchway were in the door. The door was steel, so he stood behind it and used it as a shield as he opened it.

What he didn't expect was the door to swing open suddenly with tremendous force, knocking him to the ground. Ronald's gun went flying as his assailant jumped him and brought his gun cracking down repeatedly on Ronald's head. Darkness overcame Ronald, and he drifted into unconsciousness.

Kate waited patiently for Ronald to tell her to open the door. *It shouldn't take this long to check out the basement.* She noticed that it was getting dark outside, and she went to turn on the outside light. As she did, she heard the driveway beep again. *That is probably Officer Young. He's early.*

Unbeknownst to Kate, Ronald had called for backup when he had received her call.

The assailant found rope and tied Ronald's hands and feet, although Ronald showed no signs of regaining consciousness. Quietly he went up the stairs. As he reached the top step, he called to Kate to let him in.

When the basement door opened, Kate, who was standing in front of it, backed up and let out a scream. In front of her was the man in the photo Sean had shown her the previous day. He grabbed her arm as she attempted to run. At that point, Dale, finding the kitchen door unlocked, burst into the room. Gunshots rang out as two bullets hit him in the shoulder. Down he sank with blood oozing through his shirt uniform.

Kate wrenched her arm away, causing her assailant to lose his balance. As she ran toward her bedroom, a shot went by, grazing the side of her head, causing her to momentarily lose her footing.

Inside her bedroom she quickly locked the door and ran for her bathroom. She knew it was only a matter of time before he would break down the door. She locked the bathroom door and opened the window. It was a small window, and she wasn't sure if she could make it out. She pushed out the screen and climbed up onto the small chair that she kept in the bathroom to lay her clothes on. She could hear him crashing through her bedroom door. Carefully, she shimmied out the window. As she fell to the ground, she landed awkwardly and twisted her ankle. The pain seared through her, but she knew she must run somewhere.

Kate knew she didn't have time to get to her car in the garage. Running was not an option either. Then she saw the hatch to the basement. Could it possibly be open? She tried the door and, to her relief, it opened. She quickly climbed in and locked it behind her.

It was dark inside but not too dark for her to see that the door to the basement was ajar. She quickly went in but decided that it wouldn't be a good place to hide. She saw the policeman, Ronald Greer, on the floor, tied up and motionless. A pool of blood had formed under his head. Kate debated whether she could do anything to help him and decided that she needed to call for help. Out of the corner of her eye, she saw the keys in the lock of the door to the hatch. Quickly, she removed them and went into the hatch stairwell and shut and locked the door behind her.

Then she took her phone out of her pocket and called 911. She could hardly hear the dispatcher. She didn't know whether her phone needed charging or the reception was poor because of her location. She gave her address and told the dispatcher that two officers had been injured. Not hearing the dispatcher respond, she sank down on the steps, putting her head in her hands.

Kate's ankle and head throbbed. The attacker must have heard her talking on her phone because she heard him outside yelling at her to open the hatch doors. When he received no answer, he began stomping on the metal doors. Kate knew that he couldn't shoot her through metal doors, but still she couldn't stop shaking and crying. Two brave young police officers could be dying, and she was powerless to help them.

As she sat there through his verbal assault, she dialed Sean's cell phone. She said nothing when he answered but held the phone to the hatch so he could hear the pounding and swearing. At least she hoped he could hear it. Tears streamed down her cheeks, and she began to pray.

In the distance, the wail of sirens filled the air, coming closer and closer. Kate's attacker knew he couldn't reach her and stopped banging on the doors. Cursing her, he headed to the woods.

Sean raced up Kate's driveway and saw ambulances and cruisers clustered by her garage.

Kate sat huddled in the dark against the door to her basement. Even though the stomping had stopped, she was afraid to move. She could hear quiet talking on the other side of the basement door, but the sirens had stopped. Fear had paralyzed her to the point of her being unable to do more than weep. Then she heard a familiar voice from the other side of the outside hatch doors.

"Kate, it's Sean. It's okay to open the hatch."

She almost couldn't believe her ears. She made her way, crawling up the stairs, her head and ankle throbbing. She reached up and slid the latch hook open.

Sean had the doors open and was down next to her in a minute. He could see that she had had some kind of injury to her head because blood was matted in her hair. She was in his arms, clinging for dear life. Then she passed out. He carried her up the stairs and over to waiting EMTs, who took her from him and placed her on a stretcher. Only after she was covered by a blanket did Sean go into her house.

Inside Kate's kitchen door, EMTs were readying Dale Young for transport. They had stopped the bleeding of his shoulder injury and had set up an IV to replace fluids lost from the wound. He was groggy but conscious. Sean told him that Kate was all right, and he was going to be all right too. Dale tried to tell Sean what had happened, but Sean told him there would be plenty of time for that.

After Dale was carried out, Sean went down to the basement to see what was happening there. The news was not as good. Ronald Greer had sustained a serious head injury. An IV was in place. His head had been bandaged, and he was immobilized on a stretcher.

As Sean came outside he was pleased to see that Kate was awake and sitting wrapped up in a blanket on her stretcher. Her head was bandaged, and she was drinking a steaming cup of coffee.

"How are you doing, Kate?" he asked as he crouched next to her.

"Much better now, Sean," she answered. "What about the officers who were watching out for me?"

Sean described their injuries to Kate as tears streamed down her face. Then he asked if she hurt anywhere else. She told him about her ankle. He wanted her to go to the hospital in the remaining ambulance, but she refused, so he convinced her to go with him in his car to the hospital to be checked out.

As Ronald Greer's ambulance pulled away with sirens screaming into the night, Sean helped Kate into his car. Then he went and spoke to the responding policemen and told them where he could be reached.

Once in the car, Sean gave his cell phone to Kate to call her sons. Hers needed to be charged. Michael, Elizabeth, and Andy would meet them at Memorial Hospital. On the way, Kate told him what had happened. Sean could tell how badly Kate felt about the two young officers' injuries. He tried to explain to her that it was all in the line of duty. He told her that if she hadn't called for help, all three of them might be dead.

Shortly after Sean and Kate had reached the hospital, they were joined by Kate's sons and Elizabeth. The two of them explained to her anxious children what had happened as they all waited for Kate to be checked out. Naturally, the ER doctors were busy with Ronald and Dale. Sean had spoken to the nurses at the desk, but it was too early for any word on their conditions.

At ten o'clock, Kate was taken into an examining room. The ER doctor soon came out to tell them that her head wound was superficial and wouldn't cause her any long-term problems, but they were going to X-ray her ankle to make sure that it wasn't broken since it was quite swollen.

At that point, Michael told Sean that he and Elizabeth would take Kate back to their house that night. "I should have insisted to do that initially," he said regretfully.

Sean didn't argue. He too had second thoughts about Kate staying in her home. Andy said that since he was the closest, he would take care of Nellie's cat every morning before he went to work, trying hard not to take his anger over his mother's assault out on Sean Burke.

By eleven o'clock a nurse wheeled Kate out to the waiting room. "Good news," said the nurse. "Nothing's broken, just a bad sprain. She will need to ice it and keep it elevated for a few days. We gave her a pain killer, and she can take these as needed," she said, handing Kate a pill bottle.

"Mom, you're coming home with me and Elizabeth tonight, and Andy is going to take care of Samantha tomorrow," said Michael. "I'm going to get my car and drive it up in front." The four Shaws left the hospital—the nurse pushing Kate out the hospital entrance in her wheelchair.

Sean learned that dogs had been brought in to search the woods for the suspect, with no result. They would return the next day at daybreak. Talking to the officer in charge, Sean determined that they were able to retrieve the bullet that grazed Kate's head, and it was sent off to ballistics.

Back in his car, he called the hospital and found out that Dale was in intensive care, his wife with him. He was expected to recover. Ronald, on the other hand, was on life support and not expected to live through the night.

At Michael and Elizabeth's house, Kate had finished drinking some warm milk. That and the painkiller she had been given worked together to make her drowsy. As soon as her head hit the pillow of the bed in the guest room, she was asleep.

The killer would not sleep that night. After watching the late news and hearing that an officer was clinging to life after a home invasion, he thought to himself, *Now they'll call me a cop killer. Well, they got in my way. It was them or me*. Once again he would spend the night in his recliner—gun in hand.

CHAPTER 16

Friday, June 28, 2003

Father Joe was awake early, anxious to go home. He had eaten his breakfast and had dressed. He felt a little achy, but his headache was gone. His doctor came in at eight o'clock, checked him over, and gave him permission to leave. He did warn him to take it easy for a couple of days.

Margaret was in the office when he called shortly after the doctor left his room, and Father Joe told her he could go home. She told him she would be right there. She, too, was glad he was well enough to go home.

When Father Joe did get home, he found that he was more tired than he thought he would be, and he asked Margaret to please call the priest in the next parish to cover the weekend Masses.

Before going to bed, he placed two calls—one to his brother, Tim, telling him that he was home and one to

Sean Burke. Sean was out of the office, so he left word that he was home and to return his call.

He went to bed after Irma made him a cup of tea and gave him some of his lemon squares to eat. He told her to wake him up if Sergeant Burke called. He went to bed knowing nothing about Kate's encounter with a killer.

Sean and Gerald were at Kate's house bright and early. They were part of an investigative team looking for clues as to how the suspect was able to gain access to Kate's basement.

He was at the campground bright and early, though he had parked his car down the road so as not to be noticed. He hadn't taken the time to watch the morning news He knew it would infuriate him to hear how he had failed to get to Kate. But losing his daughter wasn't all her fault, he reasoned. Patricia had some part in it. She should have stayed with him while he worked his way through tough times. She shouldn't have turned the older children against him. Hadn't he always provided for them while he had his job? He had entered the campground through the thick woods. He reflected on the fact that he had been spending a lot of his time in the woods of late. Not only were they a good place for one to observe, but they were also a good escape route. This day he would need both.

Kate woke with a start, beads of sweat on her forehead. She had been in a dream where darkness was all around her, and she was being swallowed up by a massive tornado spout. Swirling around her were things she recognized: Ted's chain saw, her desk at school, her rosary beads, a gun, her children's toys from long ago, her cell phone, and a plaid headband.

Awake now, she could feel the throbbing of her ankle, not much better than the night before. She called out for Michael and Elizabeth. When Elizabeth stuck her head in the door, Kate said weakly, "Elizabeth, I know who he is."

Looking at his cell phone, Sean knew immediately who was calling. It was Kate. When he heard her voice he could tell she was upset.

"Sean, I think I know who he is," said Kate in a quiet whisper. "I didn't recognize him without his hair and moustache."

Sean told her he'd be right over and to put Elizabeth or Michael on for directions. Within the hour, Sean, having left Gerald behind at Kate's house, was pulling in Michael and Elizabeth's driveway.

Kate was seated at the kitchen table drinking a cup of tea. She was dressed in a yellow pantsuit and a floral blouse. Her left foot, wrapped in an ace bandage, was resting on a pillowed chair with an ice pack on top of her ankle. A bandage encircled her head, covering her bullet wound. She was pale and looked tired.

Elizabeth was making her a piece of toast when Sean came to the door. Sean noticed that the table had been set for three as he entered the kitchen.

"We thought you could use a cup of coffee and a Danish, Sean," Kate said as she invited him to join her at the table. When he asked why she wasn't having a Danish, Kate told him that her stomach was a little squeamish from the pain medication.

As Elizabeth filled the coffee cup in front of Sean, Kate asked him about the wounded officers. He told her and Elizabeth that Dale would probably be released in a few days.

"And Officer Greer, Sean?" Kate asked, afraid of the answer.

"I'm sorry, Kate, he passed away during the night," Sean answered sadly. "His head injury was just too serious."

Tears streamed down Kate's face. "If I hadn't called him about the noise I heard in the basement, he'd still be alive," she said slowly.

"Now, don't go blaming yourself, Kate," Sean said. "He died in the line of duty. Besides, you or Dale Young could just as easily been have been killed by the attacker. You said you think you know his identity, Kate?"

"Believe it or not, Sean, it came to me in a dream… or a nightmare," Kate said as she took a sip of her tea. "He is a former parent of Sacred Heart. I had his youngest child, Emily, in my class. I didn't recognize him in the photo you showed me because he didn't have a moustache and long hair. Sean, somehow I feel that that little girl is in danger."

"Is that the family you and Father Joe mentioned when we talked after Al Watson was killed?" Sean asked.

"Yes, it is," answered Kate. "The last name is Lawler. Of course, I'd like you to check with Father Joe before you take my word for it." Sean told her that he planned on going to see Father Joe after he left her. He finished his coffee and left right away.

Sean called the church office from his car and was told that Father Joe was home from the hospital and was up to seeing him. The meeting would take place in the rectory. Sean knew it would be up to him to tell Father Joe about Kate's home invasion.

As he pulled into the rectory parking lot, Sean wondered how much information Father Joe would be able to give him. With priests, there was always the matter of the privacy of confession. Breaking their vow of secrecy would mean ending their priesthood. *But maybe Father Joe had enough information that he could share. Could Kate be right about little Emily Lawler being in danger?*

Irma answered the door when Sean rang the bell and led him to a small parlor where Father Joe was sitting in a recliner. He still had a rather large bandage on his forehead and was black and blue around his eyes. He also had an ugly looking scrape on his chin. Sean was surprised to see that he was not dressed in his priest clothes. He tried to remember if he had ever seen a priest without his collar.

Sean asked Father Joe how he felt. "Other than feeling like I've been run over by a dump truck, Sergeant, almost like new," the priest answered, chuckling.

"I can imagine, Father," said Sean. "Is the accident any clearer than it was before?" Father Joe told Sean that he hadn't remembered anything else.

The knock on the closed door of the parlor was Irma bringing Sean his lemonade and a plateful of Father Joe's lemon squares for them both. Handing Sean his lemonade and placing the plate on a nearby table, Irma turned to Father Joe. "I put a casserole in the fridge, Father. Just put it in the oven at 350 around 4:30 and it should be ready at 5:30," she said. "I'll be going along now. I put the phone on the service. If you need anything, call me." Father Joe thanked her, and she left for home.

"Irma is such a good soul," Father Joe said to Sean. "All she has is me and the church. She gives us both her all. We shouldn't be interrupted now."

Sean proceeded to show Father Joe the photographs of the suspect. As he expected, the priest recognized the man immediately. Then Sean told Father Joe about Kate's harrowing experience. He could see the color drain from the priest's face. Father Joe was shocked to think that both he and Kate had been targeted by this man whom he had tried so hard to help.

"Father, can you give me any idea why this man would want to hurt you or Kate or, for that matter, kill Al Watson?" Sean asked the priest.

"Without breaking any confidences, Sean, I can tell you that he was very upset about losing his job and having to take the kids out of our school. We tried to work something out to help them stay, as I told you before."

"Would you be able to tell me where to find the family now, Father?" asked Sean.

"I think a good one to ask where they moved after they left here would be Margaret, Sergeant. While they were here, she had gotten quite friendly with Mrs. Lawler."

Sean told Father Joe that he would be going up to the office to talk to her after he left the rectory. Then Father Joe invited Sean to join him for supper. "I know Irma's casserole will be delicious and will feed an army, Sergeant." For some reason, Sean got the feeling that Father Joe didn't want to be alone.

"Only if you call me Sean, Father," he answered. "I'll be able to bring you up to date on what I find out too." Father Joe thanked him, and Sean headed over to the office.

At first, Margaret wasn't too sure what she should tell Sean. She considered Patricia a friend and was reluctant to share personal information. But when Sean told her that Mr. Lawler was a suspect in Al's murder, she agreed to tell him whatever she knew.

After talking with Margaret, Sean headed back over to Kate's house to pick up Gerald. On the way, he phoned in to the station to let his office know where he would be and to find out what kind of car was registered to Edward Lawler. When he reached Kate's house, he found the forensic K9 officers packing up. Gerald was glad to see him. He told Sean that the dogs were able to follow the assailant's trail through the woods to a vacant house down the road. The theory was that he had had a car parked there, which he used for his getaway.

From there Sean and Gerald went in to town to go to lunch. Both were hungry. Sean brought Gerald up-to-date on the identity of the killer on their drive into town. They both agreed that the loss of a job and the embarrassment of withdrawing his children from their school could put a man under extreme stress, but was it enough to make him kill someone? Perhaps talking to his wife would shed some more light on his motives.

Sean was able to get an address for the Lawlers and ascertain that there were two family cars—a blue Toyota registered to Patricia Lawler and a white Saturn registered to Edward.

As they ate, Sean and Gerald debated whether to have an APB put out on Edward. They decided they would go to the address they had first and find out what they could from there.

No one was home. The lawn needed mowing, and Sean could see that there was mail in the mailbox.

As he was walking back to the cruiser, a neighbor approached him. "Officer," the woman asked. "Are you looking for the Lawlers?" Sean told her yes, and, after introducing herself, Mrs. O'Hara told Sean that they had moved. Not only that, but they had divorced. She said they had not gotten along for some time, and the bank had foreclosed on their house. She had no idea where either of them were living now but told Sean where Patricia Lawler had been working when they left. Sean thanked her for her help.

By the time Sean and Gerald reached the small dry cleaning shop in the next town, Patricia Lawler had left for the day. The owner told the officers that Patricia was an excellent worker who never was late for work or took time off. She was devoted to her children. When asked where they could reach her, her boss would only give them her telephone number because he knew she didn't want her address given out. The boss had the impression that she didn't want her former husband to know where she had relocated. Sean thanked him for his help and assured him that they had questions about her husband, not her.

Of course, when they reached the cruiser, Gerald put in a call to the station to find out the address using the phone number, and they proceeded to the Lawler house.

When they arrived, they found Patricia's car in her driveway. Sean knocked on her kitchen door. Patricia came to the door and quickly opened it. Sean could see that their presence had frightened her, so he told her right away why he was there, that he was trying to locate her former husband. She immediately invited them in.

They sat together in Patricia's small kitchen, Sean asking questions about her former husband. Patricia was cooperative and told Sean about the last two years of her life.

"Edward lost his job almost two years ago. Up to that point I thought we had a good relationship, a good family. The kids were doing well in school, we didn't have debt, Ed liked his job, and because I only worked part time, I was able to volunteer at the school. On weekends we did things as a family. After he lost his job, he seemed to change. He drank too much and was argumentative. He had no patience with the older kids. I had my part-time job and for a while, with his unemployment check, our savings, and my check, we were able to swing it. Unfortunately, he became more and more depressed as he hunted, without success, for another job. He became abusive physically and verbally. Most disturbing of all was his obsessive interest in our youngest child, Emily. I finally left him and was able to get full custody of the kids. Based on his behavior, the court ruled that he could only have supervised visits. He chose not to see the kids at all." As Patricia finished telling Sean about her husband, he could see that her eyes were brimming with tears.

"I can see this has been a difficult time for you, Mrs. Lawler. Do you think that your husband had hard feelings about taking the children out of Sacred Heart?" Sean asked.

"I know it was very difficult for him, Sergeant, admitting that he couldn't provide for his family in the way he had before," she answered. "He blamed the people at school for losing custody of the kids."

"Why would anyone at the school have been responsible for that?" asked Sean.

"He believed someone there may have reported him to the children's services as a child abuser," she answered slowly.

"And what about you, Mrs. Lawler? Did you think he abused any of your children?"

"Verbally, yes, I think he made them think, especially Emily, that they were to blame for his problems. Whoever called in thought it might be sexual abuse, but I never believed that," she answered.

Sean could see that Patricia Lawler was being as forthcoming as she could be. He wondered if she was right in her assessment of her former husband. Often in these situations, spouses are in denial when it comes to sexual abuse. They either can't, or won't, believe it's happening in their family.

Then Patricia told Sean and Gerald that her children were at summer camp and that she would need to go around 5:30 and pick them up.

Sean told her why he was looking for her husband, and although she told him that the man she knew would never kill someone, she was understandably very shaken. He advised her to keep the children home from summer camp the following week. She agreed. He gave her his card and told her to give him a call if anything came to mind or if her former husband tried to contact her. Then Sean and Gerald headed back to the station.

Sean went straight to his desk to see if he had any messages. He found that no identifiable fingerprints, other than the owner's, were found on the car that was believed to be the one that sideswiped Father Joe. He was not surprised. Paint found on the passenger side did match Father Joe's car, however. Sean wondered how Edward Lawler knew about that car being available to take. *One more thing to ask him,* he thought. He decided to ask that an APB be put out for the white Saturn owned by Lawler.

He checked and returned two unrelated messages, set up surveillance on Patricia Lawler's house, straightened up his desk, and set off for his supper date with Father Joe.

As he drove to the rectory, Sean thought he might talk to the priest about coming back to the church. Al's memorial Mass, along with Kate's evidently deep faith, were the catalysts for this decision. He missed feeling like part of the church community. He no longer was angry with God for the loss of his wife, thinking now that she was in a better place.

Sean reached the rectory at 5:15. Father Joe opened the door when he rang the bell. "I was just ready to take the casserole out of the oven, Sean."

After supper, Sean could see that the priest needed his rest, so he finished up his coffee and put all the dishes in the sink. Father Joe told him not to worry about them, that Irma would be in first thing in the morning.

Telling Father Joe that he had arranged for a plain-clothes policeman to keep a watch on the rectory for the night, Sean said his goodbyes and left with Father Joe's blessing.

As Sean went to his car, he realized that he and Father Joe hadn't talked about his return to the church. His cell phone rang as he reached his car. He didn't recognize the number but answered it anyway.

On the other end was a somewhat hysterical Patricia Lawler. "Sergeant Burke! Sergeant Burke! Emily is missing! I went to pick the kids up at camp, and they couldn't find her!" Sean told her he was on his way and headed toward the campground.

By the time Sean arrived, the camp leaders had notified the authorities and formed a search party. Patricia was in the office with her three older children. Sean could see she was very upset. Her eyes were red and tears were running down her cheeks. Her oldest son, Earl, was telling his mother and one of the camp volunteers that he had seen his sister coming back from swimming with a group of other girls her age at about

3:00. She had waved happily and continued on her way toward the building that housed the cafeteria.

Sean introduced himself to the camp volunteer and began to ask questions of Patricia and her children. None of the children had seen their father.

Patricia asked to speak privately with Sean, and the camp volunteer took her children away to get drinks and to calm them down. Patricia voiced her concern about the possibility of her ex-husband taking Emily. "I never tried to turn any of the children against him, Sergeant. The older children turned against him because of his behavior. Emily was just too young to understand fully what was going on, and he was very careful not to be abusive around her," she said quietly.

Sean asked her if she knew where Edward was living now, but she had no idea.

After assuring Patricia that her daughter would be found, he met with camp officials, telling them that he would ask for an alert. He also wanted to talk to the young people who had last been with Emily. The four young girls were brought to him. They too had seen no one but were able to tell Sean that just as they had entered the lunchroom, Emily said she had to go back outside. They assumed she had either had to go to the bathroom, which had its doors on the outside of the building, or she had forgotten something.

Phoning in the alert, Sean gave the description of Edward's car, although he was not sure if that was the car he was using.

Kate spent the day at Elizabeth and Michael's. In mid-afternoon, she gingerly got to her feet and walked to and from the bathroom, holding on to furniture and walls, trying not to put weight on her injured foot. She found that she could do so without much pain, and that thought gave her some comfort. After she had sat back in the recliner, she started going through in her mind all the encounters she had had with Edward Lawler. Other than the latest one, she had only talked with him three other times. His wife was with him each time.

She tried to recall if there were any signs that he was mentally unstable. Other than the fact that he seemed worried about Emily's performance in school the last time Kate talked to him, she couldn't pinpoint any warning signs.

Then she started thinking about Emily. Perhaps the fact that she had slipped in the quality of her work and seemed distracted at times were clues, along with the fact that she asked to go to the nurse's office more frequently than before. Kate just didn't know.

Kate tried to remember how Emily interacted with other children and felt that she had no problems there. Emily was outgoing and seemed to be a happy girl for the most part. When asked to write stories, she usually wrote about her family, friends, and animals. Any pictures she drew gave no indication of trouble at home or elsewhere. Some young children who are crying out silently for help will depict dark subjects in their artwork.

Kate had always been diligent about having her third graders share their compositions with the class. She also read each one and made storybooks with them. Emily liked writing about things her family did together. She especially enjoyed going to McDonald's with her dad. Kate picked up her phone and put in a quick call to Sean.

Kate was resting her head back in the recliner, dozing but not entirely asleep, when Elizabeth returned laden with groceries. She made her way over to the table, telling Elizabeth how much better she felt.

Norma Kelly's feet were just about killing her. She was nearing the end of a double shift at McDonald's. Normally she worked six to three on Fridays, but today a co-worker, Maureen, called in sick, and she had agreed to work until seven.

Since it wasn't overly busy right at that moment, she had taken her supper break. As she sat in the back room eating a container of yogurt, she was thinking to herself that although she prided herself on doing a good job, she was probably getting too old for this kind of work. Retired, she took this job to fill the time. Her house could only be cleaned just so much. Her children were all grown and had families of their own. Not only that, but due to their jobs they lived all over and unfortunately, not nearby.

Sitting there, she glanced at the small TV that sat across the room and noticed that an alert was coming across the screen. She couldn't hear what was being said, but did see a picture of a young girl. The youngster reminded her of one of her grandchildren. *Looks like she is about the same age,* thought Norma.

Just as she was about to go across the room to turn up the volume on the TV, Jeff, one of the other cashiers, came back to tell her that people were starting to filter in for the supper hour. She threw her yogurt cup in the trash and headed for the bathroom.

By the time Norma reached her register, lines had formed at the other two. The next customer in Jeff's line moved over to her line and placed his order. While she waited for her customer to get his money out, she glanced at the other two lines. She couldn't help but notice the bald-headed man at the end of Jeff's line. She could tell that he had a child in tow but couldn't see her face. Some of the customers in Jeff's line moved into Norma's line. As Norma was waiting on the last person in her line the man was giving Jeff his order. Standing next to him was a blonde, blue-eyed girl who couldn't have been more than nine years old. The man let go of her hand to get out his wallet, and she looked over at Norma as she put her hand in her pocket. Norma could see that her eyes were red from crying. She was dressed in a pink shirt, which had the name of a camp program, and blue shorts.

The customers dwindled, and Norma leaned over to Jeff to tell him she had to go into the back room for a minute. Once again, the TV was displaying the alert on Emily. This time, though, Norma was able to get to the TV and turn the volume up.

She decided that the little girl in the dining area looked a lot like the girl on the TV but wondered what to do about it. Norma knew that if she was wrong, things could get nasty. But what if it was the little girl they were looking for?

Quickly, Norma dug her cell phone out of her purse and jotted down the number to call on a nearby napkin. Then she went out front and told Jeff that she was going to check on the ladies' bathroom. Once inside the bathroom, she checked to see if the room was empty and then made her call.

The officer who took her call asked her a number of questions to verify where she was and whether she thought the father and child would be there for a while. Norma said that they probably wouldn't be there much longer. He said the police would be there soon but would probably be in plainclothes.

Norma went back to work. As she got behind her register, she glanced around the restaurant. Father and child were still there eating. She tried not to look in their direction and continued to take orders, wondering if he could become violent. She was focusing on a customer, handing him his change, when she looked up and saw that the man in question was standing right in front of her.

"May I help you, sir?" she asked, looking into his deep blue eyes. He ordered two sundaes, paid her, and started back to his booth.

Norma watched him and realized that the child was no longer with him. *But where could she be?* Norma asked herself. *Of course, the bathroom.*

Once again, Norma told Jeff she was going in to the ladies' room. This time she grabbed a mop and pail as if there was a plumbing problem. As she went into the bathroom, Emily was at the sink washing her hands.

"Hello," she said to the little girl. Emily looked at Norma, said hello back, and smiled.

"You look upset, was the food you got all right?" she asked Emily.

"It was fine."

"Emily, you need to hurry up," a voice boomed from the other side of the door. "Your ice cream is melting." Both Emily and Norma jumped. Emily hollered that she'd be right out.

Norma looked at that little face and took a chance. "Do you really want to go with him, Emily?" she asked.

"I don't want Daddy to get angry, but I'd rather go home to my mommy," Emily whispered to Norma.

In one motion, Norma shoved the handle of the mop through the door handle to hold it closed and took Emily's hand and led her down to the last stall, which was a roomy, handicapped one. Once inside she locked the door, knowing full well, either action would only delay the man from coming in the bathroom if he forced the issue. She held the trembling child close.

Meanwhile, Edward had started back to his seat. It was then that he saw two men out in the parking lot near his car. A chill went up his spine. *Can the police have found us already?* He wondered. He turned and went back to the ladies' room door. "Emily, come out now!" He bellowed. "We have to go!" When she didn't answer, he pushed against the door. Then he remembered seeing one of the cashiers go into the bathroom right after Emily. Edward rammed his shoulder against the door and hollered, "Open up!"

Jeff heard the commotion, came out from behind the counter, and started walking toward Edward.

"What seems to be the problem, sir?" he asked and was shocked to see that the man had turned toward him and had a gun in his hand.

Jeff screamed, "Gun! Duck!" and dove into a booth. Frantic screams abounded as parents shoved their children under tables or on the floor, many shielding them with their own bodies.

Then a man burst through the side door and, before Edward could turn and react, lunged at him, knocking him to the ground. The gun flew from Edward's hand and skidded across the floor to the booth where Jeff had hidden. Quickly, Jeff grabbed for the gun.

From the other end of the restaurant, two other plainclothes policemen came through the door and ran with guns drawn toward Edward and the first policeman, who had him pinned to the floor. Jeff came out from under his table and pointed the gun at Edward. One of the other policemen tapped him on the shoulder and said, "Nice job, sir. I'll take that gun now." Jeff handed it to the policeman, who quickly emptied the bullets into a plastic bag. The policeman who had tackled Edward put handcuffs on him and was reading him his rights. Quickly he was taken out of the restaurant to a waiting cruiser.

Jeff went to the ladies' bathroom door and called Norma's name, telling her it was all right to open the door. The door opened slowly, and out Norma came with her arm around Emily.

Slowly the patrons came out from their hiding places. A few customers came and thanked the police for their quick action and gave them statements as to what they had seen.

Officer Larry Sharp told Emily that he was calling her mother at the camp.

Sean was there in no time. With him were Patricia and her other children.

Hugs and kisses were in order. Jeff and Norma went to join Joan in making sundaes for the rest of the Lawler family.

Sean joined the other policemen in another booth, and all were quickly brought steaming cups of coffee. Once Sean was briefed by his fellow officers, he left the booth and went outside to place two calls, the first to Father Joe's answering service, the second to Kate.

It was 9:10 p.m. when the phone rang at Michael's house, "Mom, it's for you," he said as he handed the phone to his mother.

Sean said, "It's over, Kate," words that brought tears to her eyes. "He tried to take off with Emily. She's safe, and her father is in custody."

"Oh thank God" said Kate.

As they talked further, Kate asked if Father Joe knew and said that he was planning on coming over the next day. Sean told her that he had left a message for Father Joe but would call him first thing in the morning.

Sean, Kate, her children, Patricia Lawler, and her children all slept well that night.

CHAPTER 17

Saturday, June 29, 2003

At ten o'clock the next morning, Sean's car, carrying Sean and Father Joe, pulled into Michael's driveway.

Kate, Elizabeth, Michael, and Andy were waiting on Elizabeth and Michael's deck. The bright summer sun had risen in a gloriously blue sky. After all had taken seats around the deck table, Sean told them of the previous evening's events.

Edward Lawler had decided to confess rather than ask for a lawyer.

"He believed that it was Kate who had reported him to the authorities for child abuse. He claims that he would never hurt Emily in that way. After losing his job and then his family, he decided to get even with Kate by removing those he felt were important to her first. He would save her for last.

"Ted was his first victim. As Ted was going down the basement stairs, Lawler came up from behind and hit him with a baseball bat, causing his fall." Kate reached in her pocket for a tissue, took off her glasses, and wiped her eyes. Michael, tears brimming in his eyes, moved his chair closer to his mother and put his arm around her. Andy, too, moved his chair closer and put his hand on hers.

"He started following Kate and came to believe that she was close to Al. John thwarted his intent to shoot Kate next by pulling the fire alarm. In a rage, he went to her house. It was he who pulled out her paper tube. Nellie happened to be driving by and saw him do it. He broke into her house and pushed her down the stairs, hoping to kill her or at least shut her up for a while.

"After that, he began to terrorize Kate. Father Joe was next. All along he planned to kill Kate and then abduct Emily, who he believed was the only one who truly loved him. The officers at Kate's house during the home invasion were just targets Lawler thought were keeping him from getting to Kate. After that attempt failed, he gave up that plan and decided to make his escape with Emily."

"But why did he choose to go to McDonald's?" asked Michael. "You would think he would try to get away as quickly as possible."

"Possibly to put Emily at ease," answered Sean.

"How did you know to send the police there?" asked Andy.

"Your mother told me that Emily wrote frequently about family outings and that maybe he would take her there to eat before he left. We weren't sure which

McDonald's he'd go to, so we staked out all of them in a fifty-mile radius. Fortunately, Norma's call identified the correct one."

Everyone was so grateful that it was over and life could return to some semblance of normalcy.

At least for everyone except Sean, whose phone had rung with an urgent request to return to the station. Michael offered to drive Father Joe home later, and after a hug and kiss for Kate, Sean left.

Elizabeth, Michael, and Andy left Father Joe and Kate alone to catch up on school news.

"Kate, I do have a favor to ask of you," Father Joe began.

"Of course, Father," Kate answered.

"As you know, I need someone to help me with the interviewing for the new principal," continued Father Joe. "But Mary Ellen Ward is leaving for a public school job, so I need to hire a teacher too." Before she could answer, he added, "I can't think of anyone more qualified to do the interviewing than you. I just hope with all you've been through, you'd be willing to help."

Kate told the priest that she would like a few days to think about it, but in her heart of hearts she knew that she wanted to take on the job. The school had been such a big part of her life, and she felt privileged to help develop part of its future.

When Michael, Elizabeth, and Andy returned to the deck, they were all sporting large smiles. Elizabeth and Michael announced that they were expecting in January.

As Kate embraced them both, she said, "Finally, a reason to rejoice!"

After Michael had returned from driving Father Joe home, Kate told him, Elizabeth, and Andy about Father Joe's request. They had no reservations other than wanting her to get away and rest at her camper in Vermont first.

Later in the day, Kate called Father Joe and told him she would be happy to do as he had requested, but she was going to take a couple of weeks to get her house back in order and go camping.

The following Saturday, Kate, Michael, and Elizabeth left to spend a week away from it all, camping in Vermont. Andy, who couldn't get time off from work, would visit Nellie and take care of Samantha each day.

On the ride there, Kate reflected on what the future might hold and thanked God for answering prayers.